# Endorsements

Lucy Heath writes engaging narratives that draws her readers into a sense of kinship with the characters. One finds themselves entering new and exciting territories as her main characters embark on their life changing destinies. As a celebrated story teller, Heath is magnetizing! You'll find yourself looking forward to her next flow of creativity.

*LaShawna Holland-Simpson—Butterfly Living Blog-talk Radio*
*www.transformingyourlives.org*
Covington, Ga.

The novel "Matters of the Heart" by Lucy Heath is a must read for Christians who desire to read romance novels that are free from immoral gestures and language that is incompatible with ones Christian character. True Christian romance novels are a rarity. God has gifted Heath to write such novels that depict real life situations—yet keep you on the edge of your seat in anticipation of her characters next moves. I highly recommend this book to those desiring to fill their repertoire with a good read.

Bishop Nedenia P. Barber,
Founder/Pastor of—The Way Church
International & Clinical Prison Chaplin

# Matters *of the* Heart

## Seasons of Love


(Winter: The Uncertain Heart)
Lucy Heath

WestBow Press books may be ordered through booksellers or by contacting:

WestBow Press
A Division of Thomas Nelson & Zondervan
1663 Liberty Drive
Bloomington, IN 47403
www.westbowpress.com
1 (866) 928-1240



ISBN: 978-5127-8282-0 (sc)
ISBN: 978-0-578-68369-0

Library of Congress Control Number: 2017905525

WestBow Press rev. first printing - date: 06/01/2017
Reprint: A Novel Thing® - date: 05/01/2020

*To*

*Everyone who has ever gone through a season of loss and aloneness waiting to hear from God*

*I wish I could say that life is not like the scripture text in Ecclesiastes chapter three. Fortunately, or unfortunately; depending on how you view your personal situations, the Word is true. Life does have its seasons, and that includes ones love life. Some get through their season better than others. Some come out victors. Some get stuck. And others...well, they suffer heart break after heart break.*

*Love feels great when you are on the sunny side of the street; when everything's going well, and you're on top of your game, but there are some for whom that didn't happen; at least not yet, and they are the ones who may be muddling through their season of pain and an anguishing heart. It may be easy to tell them...just get over it! It's easy to say, but they must first understand the ultimate Love...Agape. Medical technology along with the help of clinical psychologist lets us know that heart break can feel very real, and may display itself in real physical emotions. The Medical name for "broken heart syndrome" is 'Takotsubo Cardiomyopathy', or another name is 'Stress Cardiomyopathy'. According to the Mayo Clinic; one may have sudden chest pain, or think they are having a heart attack because of a traumatic experience that can alter the heart rate, or making it to become irregular. While it is not directly related to one of the seasons in this novel where the character goes through sorrowful disappointments in her love life; one can determine that the agony of heart break is real, and can lead to mental, or physical issues if sustained, or goes untreated. Review Ecclesiastes, and know that there is a time to keep, and a time to cast away. Those who live a happy, healthy life are those who admit that there are some things they can't get through alone. But what if you're like the 'autumn'…* the cool chilling air that causes the *beautiful falling leaves to crackle under your feet, and each crunch reminds you of one failed relationship after another.*

*So, our characters want to know if they will ever come to know again the solace of love that now seems to wane from them. Yes, waning even in the love they once had for the Lord? Is this a passing season, or do they just settle in and accept their fates of happenstance?*

**To that question; the Lord answered…**

*To everything there is a season, and a time to
every purpose under the heaven:*

*A time to be born, and a time to die; a
time to plant, and a time to pluck up that
which is planted;*

*A time to kill, and a time to heal; a time
to break down, and a time to build up;
A time to weep, and a time to laugh; a
time to mourn, and a time to dance;*

*A time to cast away stones, and a time to
gather stones together; a time to
embrace, and a time to refrain from
embracing;*

*A time to get, and a time to lose; a time
to keep, and a time to cast away;*

*A time to rend, and a time to sew; a time
to keep silence, and a time to speak;*

*A time to love, and a time to hate; a time
of war, and a time of peace.
He hath made everything beautiful in his
time: He hath set the eternity in the heart
of men…*

*I know that, whatsoever God doeth, it shall be forever: nothing can be put to it; nor anything taken from it: and God doeth it, that men should fear before him.*

*Ecclesiastes 3:1-8, 11a, 14*

# Winter
## The Uncertain Heart

"Where do you go from *Happily Ever After*"?

# Chapter 1

Without a doubt, this was the most daunting, the most unlikely thing Beverly had ever done since her husband's death. But it was time; no, it was past time. She had to come out of her grief and start a new life for herself. For the last almost five years she had lived her life through her children, and other friends. Ronald died almost five years ago this past Thanksgiving, and it was at this year's family gathering that Beverly would announce her new plans—at least the one that she thought would help her to face the future *of* Beverly.

Of course, her children all wondered if she was okay, if anything was wrong. No one said it out loud, but they probably were wondering if she had lost her mind. She assured them everything was all right—that she just decided it was time for her to do something different. *No*, she didn't want anyone to go with her. And, *yes* she would e-mail them all the information they needed to have before she left, including her itinerary. And *yes*, she would be perfectly safe. And, *No*, for the second time, she didn't want anyone to go with her.

What she didn't tell them was, as much as she loved her grown children, they couldn't fill the empty bleakness inside her heart. Only God could do that. She just wanted to get away, to take a sabbatical so she could hear from God… *Love* on Him, and allow Him to love on her. Beverly admitted to herself that letting God love on her was something she had refused to do over the past few years. She shut God out from doing that, or at least she tried. Now that she stopped blaming Him for taking her husband away and leaving her a widow, she wanted to once again feel the fullness of God's adoring love.

------------~------------

Beverly left the Thanksgiving gathering that evening wondering if she had done the right thing. Maybe she shouldn't go alone. Would it be safe for a woman of her age to travel by herself? Would a stranger be watching every move she made? Doubt began to enter in, and cause her to wonder if she had made a *wise* decision. She had been listening to her children all evening, and all three of them had their own reasons why she shouldn't go alone. As a matter of fact, Emily, the eldest, didn't think she should go at all. Carol, the youngest, didn't oppose it; except she *was* concerned about her mother traveling alone. Not in particular about her safety, but because this would have been the first time she had ventured out by herself.

In the past she had traveled to a few places in the United States, visiting relatives and such, but that was when she was still married. Beverly thought, *yes when I still had Ronald.* Carol questioned why her mother had chosen to go out of the country instead of choosing to go to one of those resort get-a-ways. But Beverly didn't want that. She wanted to leave the country; maybe by doing that, she could leave behind her oncoming depression too.

Fortunately Beverly had already begun to put up her Christmas decorations. She wasn't concerned about turning on the stationary Christmas lights on the outside of the house. Ronald Junior was more than willing to come over to check the strand over the hedges for blown out bulbs that were already in place from previous years. This year she told him no. For one thing, she was going to be out of town, and didn't want lights burning outside the house during the day. The security lights on the outside of the garage were motion detectors, and the light over the front door would come on at dusk. Timers were on the kitchen light, and on the lamp in one of the front bedrooms upstairs. She was not only thinking of the electric bill, but also of how unnatural it would look for her to change things around from the normal daily routine.

Since she was leaving on December 22, the family wanted to have Christmas with her at her house on the weekend before she left. That meant the house would be full of people. Beverly thought; *I love my children and grandchildren. I love my son-in-law and my daughter-in-law; but I'll have to lay down some rules first.*

Rule number one was, she wasn't going to be doing any cooking, or extra cleaning up that would wear her out. Having five adults and five children to entertain for two whole days could be exhausting. She explained to them that the cruise was *her* Christmas present to *herself*, and she didn't want to be too tired to enjoy it. The second thing was that they could have all the fun and eating they wanted, as long as the house was put back in order when they left. Beverly had completed all of her Christmas shopping, and had planned to deliver everyone's gifts on the weekend of the twentieth.

Now, everything was getting blown out of proportion. But she guessed that's the way the holidays go. As much as she wanted to, she wasn't going to put up a tree this year, but now that the grandchildren were going to be there, their parents wanted to have a tree. *Why, I don't know,* Beverly thought? They already had a tree at their house—at least everyone did but Carol. She was going over to her sister's house for the

Christmas. Carol taught in the public school system, and they were going to be off for two whole weeks.

The kids opted out for one of those 4 foot trees you could place on a stand, or a tabletop. They made themselves satisfied with that. They decorated it with a few ornaments they picked off of their own trees from home. One strand of twinkle lights did the trick, and the tree looked beautiful. Emily and Ronald said it was mine to keep just in case in the near future I didn't feel like putting up a big tree.

They knew how much I love the Christmas season, and they wanted me to have something to brighten my spirits when I returned from my trip. Besides, the tree was a one-step process to put up and take down, it would be easy to do. That way I wouldn't have to fool with dragging a big old tree in the living room every Christmas; that is if I didn't want to. Wisdom let me read between the lines, and what I heard was that … *Ronald and his brother-in-law wouldn't have to drag a big live evergreen tree in and out of the house for me every year.*

Beverly loved the smell of a fresh cut Christmas tree. She always had, but he was right. Her husband had done that for her for the past twenty-six years of their married, and after that, it fell on Ronald Junior to keep up the tradition. She must have never thought about it in that way. Well, if she could break with tradition and spend Christmas day away from her family on a cruise, she guessed she could get used to this little table-top tree. Beverly thought she just might forego the big tree for next year, and use the little tree from now on. She wasn't in the mood for dragging Christmas trees in and out of doors anyway.

# Chapter 2

Having two Christmases sounded great to the grandchildren. It was their parents who were complaining. Beverly tactfully reminded them that it was their idea to have two Christmas celebrations, not hers. They were the ones who had to have the pictures and videos of the children opening their presents at grandma's house on Christmas morning. Then there was the expense of having two dinners. Beverly told them she was okay just having the *'tree* scene ', but they wanted to have the whole thing—dinner and all the trimmings for their camera phones. It didn't seem to matter one way or the other to Carol, but maybe that was because she was single and didn't have any children.

Emily was the perfectionist. She had to have everything *picture perfect.* She was also the one who did the most complaining. Evidently she and Ronald had been talking. They were the ones who had children. He told her they just couldn't afford the expense of two Christmases.  So Beverly suggested that they forego the second big dinner and use the remaining turkey and ham for their own Christmas dinner. After all, it was only in four more days and all they would have to do was to add fresh side dishes. Maybe, if she wanted to, Emily could bake another cake and a sweet potato pie. That way, their picture wouldn't be ruined by slices and chunks that had been taken from the other desserts. You might've thought she asked her daughter to do something dishonorable. Beverly knew the true reason behind Emily's actions was that she was hurt that her mother would—of all things– choose a "*sacred*" time like this to be 'selfish' enough to do something for herself, and not think of the family. Beverly knew her children well, and what Emily really wanted to say, or at least what she felt–was that her mother had ruined it for everybody. She had ruined *their* Christmas!

Working past attitudes, putting aside pride, and mustering up a little more faith, they were able to have a good pre-Christmas celebration for the weekend. Since she had given them almost one-month notice before the cruise, her children were innovative enough to come up with gifts she could take along with her. Beverly had spoken to one of her girlfriends from church who had been on two cruises. She advised her to pack light. She said she had made the mistake of packing everything but the kitchen sink on her first cruise—a change of clothes for twice a day, and shoes and jewelry to go with everything. She brought along most of her toiletries, a flat iron and hair rollers, snacks (*she said those probably would needed*) and everything else that made her feel like she hadn't left home. It was only a four-day cruise, and she had packed her husband's bags the same way.

Penny said they had far too many pieces of luggage to carry by themselves, so they ended up paying out extra money to have someone to help carry the overload. She said she spent too much time every day trying to decide what to wear, and besides that—her husband didn't wear half the things she packed for him. Plus the poor thing had to buy an extra piece of luggage to get the things home she shopped for at the different ports. By the time she went on her second cruise, Penny said she had learned her lesson. Why packed the house if you're trying to get away from home!

"Honey, she told her, pack like you're going on the Mission field. Put as much as you can in one suitcase, stuff the rest in your carry-on." bring along a nylon tote bag for all the extra shopping."


RJ (Ronald Sparks Junior) said he took one of the original gifts back to the store that he brought, and got his mother something a little more practical for her excursion—a Tablet. He said there were more up to date, advanced electronics out there on the market, but he knew her and gadgets. So, he thought the one he chose would be something she could handle. Carol chipped in to pay for her mother's first 12 months of service as one of her gifts to her. They spent an hour or two working with Beverly to make sure she knew how to send and receive e-mails, take and send photos to their phones, e-mail them, and work the Internet. They said she probably wouldn't get my Internet service out on the high seas, but she could take endless pictures of everything. Beverly even learned how to *Skype*. But the best thing about the weekend was she felt that they were easing into accepting that *maybe* she could began to live my life again without their help. They had to learn how to let go. And so did Beverly, and this was as good a time as any to try.

---

Thomas had a hard time convincing his dad that doing something different for Christmas would help lift him out of his sluggish stupor. Brandon Woods was a land man. He told his family over and over again, he didn't want to fly anywhere, and he's certainly didn't want to sail on no doggone boat! Wherever he wanted to go, he could take a car, a bus, or the train. Before he was widowed, he planned—*they* planned on doing so much together when he retired from Amtrak. He started working for the company when he was only twenty-four years old, and he married Grace one year later. So, retiring at age 55, he was still a pretty young man. Grace was such a beautiful woman. She was a caring mother, and a loving wife. It just didn't seem fair. He was the one who rarely watched his diet and did even less exercise—yet right after they celebrated their 29th wedding anniversary, Grace complained of not feeling well, not up to par.

It made Brandon angry every time he thought about how it was possible for someone to get annual checkups, mammograms, and whatever else it is that women get checked out for—still after of all of *that*, cancer slips in and takes a beautiful life. *Here I am* he thought, almost *three years later still alive. I'm the one she almost had to beat over the head with a stick, to go in for checkups.*

Brandon had started to become bitter and grumpy. He didn't really notice it until his son pointed it out to him. Thomas was right. Brandon complained about everything. So it was understandable that he withdrew from most of the social activities he and Grace used to attend together with their friends—*their married friends.* Now-a-days he felt like a square peg trying to fit in their old round circle of friends. Actually, he had begun to resent their happiness. He would see women every day that didn't look like they took care of themselves. Their bodies were out of shape, they were overweight, and some of the elderly ones had to steady themselves with a cane, but they were still here living and enjoying life. *Come back Gracie and enjoy life with me like we used to. I miss you so much.*

---

Beverly switched-out some of the things she had previously packed in her carry-on bag for some of the new things she received from the kids. One of the things she packed was the satin nightgown that Emily had given her. Her daughter told her since she was trying new things; she might as well try satin. Beverly removed one of the nightgowns from her bag. She took a good look at it. Without really knowing it, her daughter was right. What she removed looked like something you would give to a bride on her wedding day—*something old, something borrowed, and something blue.* Beverly had to laugh at herself for making it sarcastically funny. She hadn't bought any new lingerie since Ronald died, and what she did have, she bought years before his death. *Her previous thought was— what does it matter? It's not like anyone's ever going to see me anyway.* Now, she began to rethink about the way she thought of herself. She envisioned herself wearing the satin PJs with her new peek-a-boo step-in slippers, and she liked what she saw.

Beverly was glad it was Carol who drove her to the airport. She didn't know why, but here lately she felt closer to her baby girl then she did to the other children. Maybe it was because they both were single, or maybe it was because she seemed to be more on Beverly side then the older ones. She thought it was kind of cute that Carol, in her sly way, was trying to give her some pointers on the opposite sex. She had no idea that her mother was going on the cruise just for herself–not to meet some Joe 'blow', or John Doe. Beverly thought to herself, *I already had my love. I didn't have any real complaints about my marriage. I was a good wife, an almost great mom, and now, a pretty good grandmother. I can't say my marriage was a 'Cinderella' story because at the end of it—my prince died. But, still it was great, and anyway... Where do you go from "Happily ever after"?*

Carol warned her mother again not to give her Tablet phone number, out to people she hardly knew, but it was all right to give them her email address. Beverly didn't know where these kids think they got all this good advice from in the first place.  They didn't raise themselves!

Carol made her mother repeat her email address several times to see if she'd remembered it. Her children put their e-mail addresses in her Tablet. So later, all she would have to do was go to the e-mail icon of my provider, click and look for the symbol to "send". They told her when she touched it, the keyboard would automatically come up. Then, as soon as she touched the first couple of letters in their e-mail address, the whole thing would show up on the bar. Today's technology is fabulous, she thought, but still she wrote down the instructions and all of their e-mail addresses on a little piece of paper and stuck it in my makeup bag.

# Chapter 3

'*This is the stupidest thing I have ever heard of*'. Brandon had his open suitcase on the bed. Of course Thomas was anxious to go on this cruise, *he thought*, and why not? He's thirty-two years old, divorced, and looking to "*swing*" a little; but that's not for me. *I was used to being with one woman for thirty years. What am I supposed to do on a cruise vacation*? If it weren't for the advertisement in the cruise brochure, Brandon probably wouldn't be going at all. But, the warm tropical breezes, the crystal blue-green waters, and the six meals a day the brochure boasted about were enough to convince him to go. Brandon could have cared less about the ship's clubs and night life, and when he looked into the extra cost of the excursions; well, he decided the things that were happening on board the ship were good enough for him.

*Whoever heard of going on a vacation at Christmas time?* Who wants to be spending time with strangers, when they could be spending time with family and friends? Brandon stuffed some more things into his suitcase. He stopped to think about what just ran through his mind. He had been so critical and grumpy lately; maybe family didn't want to be around him at this joyous time of year. And as for friends—well, he had shunned most of the ones he and Gracie had associated with. But not because he disliked them, it just hurt too much to be reminded of how happy he once had been. Brandon's eyes began to moisten as he had to admit to himself how much he struggled to come out of his grief. Maybe his son thought this cruise would somehow help.

———————— ∼ ————————

No matter how Melvin tried to fix it up in his mind, if the truth be told he was no better than a sneak, a spy, and worse than the other two names he called himself, he was a *'peeping'* Tom. It sounded like a good idea when Emily first suggested it to him. The idea of being on a cruise with Beverly was the chance of a lifetime.

Emily was concerned about her mother traveling alone, and she wanted to be sure her mom was safe. She knew *Mr. Melvin* was one of the men her dad had been buddies with. He owned two auto repair shops. Though he was the sole owner and proprietor (so far she knew) his son and nephew managed the two shops now. Mr. Melvin said when he turned fifty he had put in enough years of labor.

Then he wanted to take it easy and let the younger folks run things. He divorced several years ago, and that's what drew him back to the church.

Aside from working on their family cars, he became friends with Mr. Sparks. Several guys from the church became a circle of close knit friends. One guy was a high school friend, and the other worked for Mr. Melvin at his shop. They got together once a week to play cards—Gin Rummy, Bid Whisk, and Twenty-one. Emily's mother and the other wives would allow them their 'men's night out; and the ladies (the ones who were married) would do something every once in a while, like meet for lunch or go to the Mall.

Melvin reflected on Emily's offer to pay for his cruise, but he was glad he said 'No'. He said he was a family friend, and that was the least he could do for her mom—in memory of her dad.

Melvin knew that the ship was a massive transport vehicle and it held thousands of passengers and crew members. Yet, he had the distinctive feeling he wouldn't be able to avoid bumping into Beverly before he wanted to. He knew he couldn't spend the whole time in his cabin, or else, how would he be able to keep an eye on her? He didn't take this *so called* assignment to satisfy Emily's conscience. He agreed because he knew within his heart, he harbored feelings for Bev for a long time. Emily gave him all of her mother's travel information, including her cabin number.

Melvin didn't want to admit that he had begun to have feelings for his friend's wife–*after all*, all of them were respectable Christians. He remembered being befriended by Ronald when he came back to the *church* after his divorce.

One Sunday after the morning service ended they were in the vestibule and Ronald mentioned something about needing to take his car into a mechanic because it was making a strange noise. That's when he found out that Melvin had a repair shop, and he became their family's mechanic. Melvin was invited to Sunday dinner a couple of times, and then was invited to come over on a Friday evening for a friendly game of cards—no gambling, just guy talk and good food. He never thought then how much he looked forward to those fellowships, and had not noticed how much he was being healed from the emptiness of his divorce.

He *surely* didn't recognize that he began to look forward to seeing Beverly just as much as he looked forward to the comradely of his new found friends. It just slipped into his realization after one of those Friday evening visits, and he did all he could do to dismiss the feelings. He thought about the times he excused himself from joining the group on some of those weekends, saying he had a job to finish up. He would say the customer needed his, or her car by Saturday morning. Melvin didn't mean to lie to his friend, but it was better than telling him the truth. *I think I'm in love with your wife.*

Once Beverly approached the boarding process and got through it all, she was glad Carol had drilled her over and over again on what was going to happen. She was thankful she kind of halfway new what to look for, and what to expect. Beverly just wished pictures weren't taken of you as soon as you boarded the ship. After running through an airport, catching a plane, the cruise shuttle over to the ship, and going through customs—one would have to wonder what that picture would look like. But, she smiled anyway.

The next challenge she had to accomplish was to find her cabin. It took a little more walking than Beverly had expected, so she was thankful that she only had her handbag and her cosmetic case to carry. The kids let her know that by the time the ship would pull dock and they were under way; her other luggage would be sitting at her cabin door some time before dinner.

The ship was humongous. Beverly began to wonder if she had made a big mistake by not starting out with a three or four day cruise. She remembered searching the Internet, and checking with her travel agency, but none of those cruises included the Christmas holiday package. Finding her cabin, Beverly slid the plastic key card down into the slot and pushed down on the handle. She flipped on the switch, and light flooded the semi-large room. The cabin was exactly as the brochure had pictured it. Her eye caught something on the small round table near the corner next to the vanity. What? A smile lit her face. *You mean to tell me this cruise line puts flowers in your room?*

Beverly laid her things on the bed, and went over to take a closer look at the bouquet of white lilies and red roses. The bouquet even had sprigs of Douglas fir, cedar, and Holly in it. Beverly leaned closer and took in the aroma of Christmas. She was smiling like a kid on Christmas morning. She lifted the note card from the bouquet. It was from the kids. *"Bon voyage and happy Christmas"!* Well bless my soul; she thought, this may be an enjoyable venture after all.

————— ∿ —————

Melvin sat in his cabin, which was three doors down and across the corridor from Beverly's. His mind was engulfed in a conundrum of emotions. He was grateful he had not accepted Emily's offer to pay for his cruise. He paid for the cruise and his own airfare, but he still felt like a heel. He wished he had thought this thing through before accepting her offer. But, he was so anxious to jump at the chance to be close to Beverly, he just didn't stop to think. Even when making reservations, he had to try and get a cabin located on deck 10 where Beverly was, or otherwise how would he be able to track her comings and goings? The bad part about it was that it was virtually impossible for them not to bump into each other. Emily might have been trying to do her mother a favor, but Melvin *knew* the feelings he had for Emily's mother—Emily didn't.

He looked down at his 'ship-n-sail' pass. He had the early dinner seating in the Flamingo dining room. The main dining rooms were only one deck up. Melvin could take the stairs if he wanted to. He wasn't sure if Beverly had boarded yet or not. He had to take his chance on getting two decks up without being seen by her if she had already checked in. Since the ship wouldn't pull dock for another forty-five minutes to an hour, he could still use his cell phone to make a call.

The strain of being a *Peeping Tom* was already too much for him. It had only been a couple of hours, but he had to get in touch with Emily and call the whole thing off. Passengers had started to gather on deck. The '*Grill*' (the outside cafeteria style food area) was open and serving hamburgers, hot dogs and French fries.

Melvin strolled over to the far end of the open exit area. He saw some heavy plastic swag strips covering the exit to an outside observation deck. He stood by the railing. He dialed Emily's number. *Why do people have cell phones, and never answered them?* He hated talking to voicemail. He wanted to talk to a person; especially *this* one. This was the kind of thing that required a personal conversation–not a voicemail. He hung up and decided to dial her number again in a few minutes. Maybe she was on the phone with someone else and was just hanging up.

He redialed and got voicemail again. He didn't want it to go this way, but he would just have to leave her a message, and hope she would call him before the ship got too far out into the waters. He waited for her voicemail message to end, waited for the beep, and then was just about to leave his message when a somewhat familiar female voice coming from behind him said: "Melvin, Melvin Blake. Of all the people in the world to find on a cruise ship. Is that you?" He froze dead in his tracks.

# Chapter 4

Beverly was glad Emily called her before the ship pulled dock. She had just hung up from Carol, and told her she received the flowers. The cruise line left a small box of European chocolates in a beautifully wrapped box that had a Christmas ornament on top of it. There was a small bowl of fruit from the travel agency, and a bottle of complimentary champagne on ice. She told Emily she didn't know who that could have come from since they knew she didn't drink, but she was going to try a little and give a toast to herself. When Beverly spoke with Emily she told her she got a little nervous trying to remember how to get RJ's e-mail, but she even surprised herself and went through the process like a champ.

When she hung up from her daughter, Beverly took the initiative to find her way up to the open deck. She knew she didn't have anyone to wave goodbye to, she just wanted to experience the view of actually leaving the coastline of the United States and heading out to sea. Beverly didn't want to appear old-fogeyish, or look like a first-time cruiser. After all, she was on a cruise ship leaving from Florida, but it still was the month of December. So she grabbed the shrug she had worn on the plane, and carried it in the crock of her arm just in case the weather was a little breezy. She slipped her 'Sail-n-Board' pass in her petite cross-over body bag, and headed up the stairs.

--------------------~--------------------

Brandon set on the edge of one of the two single beds in their cabin. Thomas was more than ready to get his fun cruise underway. He said he was going to go top-side and check things out. Brandon knew what his son meant by '*things*'. He took out one of the brochures from the "Welcome Aboard" package, and  told Thomas he wanted to familiarize himself with the ship first before he started roaming around.

He actually felt his nerves churning around in his stomach, but he couldn't let his son know that. He already knew that a few sips of ginger ale would help to settle his stomach, but he didn't want to venture out until he knew exactly where he was going. Having glanced through the brochure, Brandon checked for his wallet in his back pocket, and decided to take the stairs to the top level. He patted the little bulge that was beginning to form around his mid-section. It

was feeling a little queasy. The snack bar
and the *'Grill'* were only three decks up, and
this was as good a time as any to begin a
little exercise. If he was lucky he could get
something from there to quiet the churning
in his stomach.

Brandon went to the 'Grill's' counter.
He didn't mind paying for the Ginger Ale if
he had to, however the bartender gave him to
Ginger Ale free of charge. Maybe it was
because he knew why Brandon needed it. He
took his drink and sat at one of the many
vacant tables lining the deck. Just about that
time, the ship began to move. He sat with his
back facing the glass observation area. He
didn't want to take any chances on ruffling
his already upset stomach by watching
streams of water, or waves whisk by the
ship.

~

The ship had begun to move, so
Beverly quickly maneuvered to the closest
table and sat with her bowl of fresh cut fruit
and her cup of coffee. She wasn't feeling
seasick or nauseous, she just had to get a
grip on the image of standing still while
things you appear to be moving. It was sort
of like when you're parked in your car and
you're getting ready to back up. You put the

car in reverse with your foot still on the break, but the car next to you starts moving out of its parking spot, and because it gives you the illusion that your car is moving too, you push down even harder on your breaks.

Beverly sat and took a few sips of her coffee to settle her nerves before turning to look out of the expansive observation windows. Yelp! They were moving all right. She thought she would finish her fruit and coffee before going out near the railing to watch the ship move into the open waters. Just then she looked to her left and saw a man sitting a couple of tables over from hers. He looked to have been in his early to mid-fifties. He wasn't a bad looking man, he just looked a little queasy. Beverly wondered if she had any of those pills with her you take for sea sickness. Yes. There were some in her little bag.

The gentleman was sipping from what could have been a glass of tonic water–or then again, it could have been Gin, or even Ginger ale.  They all were clear drinks. Beverly wondered if she should be so bold as to offer him a couple of her pills. Her old passive, reserved self was telling her to mind her own business, but her new adventurous self said, *"I thought you wanted to change your hum-drum life. Go ahead! What could it hurt?"* Beverly placed a napkin over her plate, and pushed back from the table.

Just as she stood, another woman appeared to be heading toward the gentleman's table. Beverly almost sat back down, and then noticed that the woman continued on past his table. Still standing there she thought, *what if he's married, and what if his wife is on her way to join him right now?*

Again, pessimism set in. I don't want to make any trouble for anyone. *This is stupid!* She almost sat for the second time when the gentleman looked her way and gave her a smile. It was a friendly, sort of pasty smile—*nonetheless*, a smile. Girding up her courage she said out loud, "Well here goes."

Beverly walked the few steps to his table. She introduced herself, apologized for interrupting his privacy, and then asked if he felt all right. He admitted that he was feeling a bit on the queasy side. Beverly said she had some Meclizine tablets, and he was more than welcomed to have some. She didn't know why she felt the need to caution him against the use of alcohol when taking them, but she did. She said if he hadn't taken any pills before he began travel, he should rest for an hour before any other activity.

She immediately felt a blush of embarrassment come over her face. She didn't know if this man was married or not, and here she was acting like his '*Momma*'. Activity to him could have meant something different than it did to her.

"I didn't mean—well, what I meant to say was…" She could tell the gentleman was a little embarrassed too, but he smiled anyway and said, "No need to be explain, I know what you meant, and just to show you I'm a good patient, I'm going to take these right now."

He swallowed the two tablets and followed up with a few gulps of whatever it was he had in his glass. Hopefully it wasn't alcohol. Brandon caught Beverly's eyes as they followed the drink glass to his lips. He finished the drink and set the glass on the table. "By the way he said…tapping his index finger on the glass, this is Ginger Ale." Beverly was so embarrassed for staring at his lips while he drank, she started to turn and leave. Brandon quickly stood and said, "Thank you Beverly Sparks. You have been a Florence Nightingale to *one* desperately in need of medical attention. Thanks for coming to my rescue." She lowered her head, and started back to her table. Brandon called out to her.

"By the way, my name is Brandon Woods."
Beverly turned to say,
"Pleased to have met you Brandon Woods,
and I hope you enjoy your cruise, and have a
Merry Christmas." He thanked her again for
the pills, and went to his cabin to lie down.

———————— ～ ————————

Melvin turned to see Anita Brown—as
he last knew her, looking straight in his face.
Anita was an old classmate of his. They all
had aged over the past twenty-five years, but
she was still a strikingly beautiful woman.
He had not gone to the last two class
reunions because of his divorce, but he
remembered seeing Anita at the reunions
that he did attend.

The look of shock and surprise must
have still been on his face. Anita spoke
again. "Surprised? I know I am." Melvin was
blown away, and said something silly like,
"What are you doing here?" "Me, she said?
What are you doing here? You are the last
person I would have ever expected to see on
a cruise." "Well, he said, people do change."
Melvin thought to himself: *What else was I
going to say; that I was snooping on my
good friend's widow—that I was a peeping
Tom?* Anita was saying, since it was yearly
long waits between class reunion times,

some of the girlfriends who stayed in touch with each other decided to go on a cruise.

Melvin excused himself from their conversation for a moment saying he had to make an important phone call. The ship was underway—close enough to the main shore where he still *had* to reach Emily. He stepped out of earshot from Anita, and hit the re-dial button. Anita said she would catch up with him later, maybe at dinner. She said she had the second seating. Melvin was so on edge, he would have to check his '*pass*-card' again to see which seating he had. But there wasn't time for that now. The other line picked up, and he could only hope that Emily would understand, and all wouldn't unravel once he told her his plans.

His conversation with Emily was quick, and straight to the point. He couldn't go through with the way she had originally planned things. He didn't want to have to tell a lie if he ran into her mother. He told her if that happened, he would feel much better telling her the truth. And, *that* particular truth was that his feelings for her went deeper than being just a close friend of the family. That when he heard that she was cruising alone–he felt this was a chance for him to express his feelings for her, and maybe they could get to know each other better.

"What? What?" Emily repeated herself again. "Hello. Mr. Melvin, are you still there?" She said a few unpleasant words. Melvin knew their communication was fading, because he was only picking up every other word that she was saying. So he quickly said, "Sorry 'bout our deal. Goodbye, I'll talk to you when I get back." He was almost grateful the line was dropped. He powered-down his phone, and stuck it in his pocket. Not wanting to loiter around on deck, he went down the stairs and headed toward his cabin.

He was already peeping and peering over his shoulder looking out for Beverly. *See*, he said to himself, *that's exactly just what I didn't want to spend my time doing.* "I've got to get back to my cabin, he said aloud, to figure this whole thing out. I need to figure out what I'm going to say to Beverly should we accidentally meet up with each other."

Melvin closed his cabin door behind him and sat on the bed thinking how strange it was that he should run into Anita. *Maybe*, he thought, *it's not so strange after all. As a matter of fact it's kind of ironic. She may very well be the excuse I need for being here.*

 In the meantime, Melvin wondered if he needed to change the time for his dinner seating.

# Chapter 5

Beverly was really excited. She couldn't believe she was really on a cruise ship. She wanted to go back to the cabin and change into more comfortable shoes before she started checking things out, but she was already lost. She took the elevator down two decks, so why did she end up in another part of the ship? Okay, maybe her floor began one and a half levels down. But how, she wondered do I get to that point. She also felt that she was walking in the opposite direction of where she needed to go in order to find her cabin. And now, an announcement was coming over the PA system for all passengers to report to their Munster stations. She had no idea what they were talking about. Did she hear them say something about lifejackets? What in the world was going on? She told herself to remain calm and not to panic. She thought, *why didn't I read the brochure that had the layout of the ship on it?*

Being composed wasn't working very well. Now, she had to go to the bathroom. Luckily she spotted a crew member who not only pointed her in the right direction of the nearest facility, but by looking at her 'ship-n-sail' pass, was able to direct her to the deck her cabin was on. The announcement said this was only a drill, and passengers did not need to put on their lifejackets, but all passengers were to get to their Munster stations as soon as possible. Beverly brought along with her the part of her information packet that outlined the ships decks, and highlighted all of its venues, restaurants, featured food areas, spas, clubs, and shops.

The test drill was over, and the first dinner seating was in about an hour and a half. Beverly was hungry, but she wanted to find the Flamingo Dining Room before she went back to her cabin to freshen up. The map of the ship was very helpful. It made her feel a bit more confident and secure about where she was going. The shops aboard ship were not open yet, but she browsed down through that section anyway. Everything was so beautifully decorated.

On her way back to her cabin, she passed through one of the casinos, and a little ways down from that was a nightclub. It wasn't open yet, but she was drawn to the entrance when she heard the Christmas music playing. She didn't know if it was piped throughout the entire ship, or just in that specific club. The room was larger than she expected, and it had a white baby grand piano in it. You really didn't get the feeling that you were on a cruise ship.

The room was empty except for the crew
preparing for its opening this evening.

Beverly stood for a moment to listen to
the music. "*Silver bells*"; one of her favorite
holiday songs was playing. She didn't mind
that it was a secular Carol. She expected that
most of the ones she would hear on board
would be that type. That didn't bother her any.
She loved just about any song of the season;
secular or sacred. She wasn't that much of a
religious prude. Singing "*Silver Bells*" or "*I'm
dreaming of a White Christmas*" didn't cause
her faith to become shaky, nor her love for God
to dwindle.

Standing at the opening, her mind took her
back to the years she and Ronald shopped together
for the kids Christmas presents. They had so much
fun going from store to store. They made those trips
their date nights. The grandparents would come
over to watch the children while they went to dinner
or a movie. They chose one or the other because
they were Christmas shopping and did not want the
night to be too strenuous on their folks. Their folks
loved their grandkids, but it had been a while since
they had to tend to small children, and she and
Ronald didn't want babysitting to be a burden on
them. Beverly vaguely heard a voice saying; "*Miss.
Miss, are you all right? Is there anything that you
need?*"

Beverly came out of her musing and focused
her eyes on the figures standing in front of her.

"Excuse me", she said. "Are you all right Madame?" The crew attended repeated himself. It was then that Beverly realized she had a fixed smile on her face, but her cheeks were stained with tears. "May I get you a drink of water, or maybe you'd like to come in and sit for a minute." Beverly shook her head *no*. "No thank you. I'm alright. Really, I just… I just." She thought *how silly I must look.*

Beverly collected herself and headed straight for her cabin. She sat in the chair beside the small desk staring at the Christmas plant and wondered if she was really ready for this voyage, or should she have waited. She wasn't quite sure what she would be waiting on—her kids were all grown adults, she was still a widow, and Ronald *still* wasn't coming back—*ever*. She looked at the champagne on the dresser. *Yes,* she thought, *I will have some, but not right now. Not while she was feeling down and depressed. That would be the wrong move to make for someone who has a temperament like mine. No. I'll wait until I'm feeling upbeat and positive.* Beverly had to pull herself together.

Right about then she didn't feel very sociable. She read through the little newsletter that was in the cabin when she arrived. There wasn't much going on for the first night on board, although there was a meeting in the 'Palace' theater for all of those who wanted to become more acquainted with the ship. There would also be one tomorrow morning.

The day had already been long and tiring, so she thought she would go to the 'Breezes of the Sea' (the larger self-serve cafeteria style dining area) for dinner, instead of going to the formal dining room for her scheduled seating. By the time she worked her way through the salad section, she realized her plate was full. *Now,* she thought, *I'm going to look like a pig carrying two plates of food.*

Beverly chose a table near the bay windows where she could look out at the ocean. The soft rippling waves seemed to calm her spirit. She was hoping her suitcases would have been delivered to her cabin by the time she returned. She took her time looking around the immaculate setting and enjoyed listening to the low toned chatter of the dining passengers. When she decided to stay a little longer, she went to get a little dessert and to refill her glass of tea. Just that fast she lost her bearings, and was trying to remember which direction she came from. Looking out of the corner of her eye she thought she caught a glimpse of a familiar looking face. Seeing her table, Beverly took a few steps in that direction, but stopped to look around the area again. The room was very large, but the man with the familiar looking face had disappeared.

*Anyway,* she thought—*how many times have people traveled somewhere and run up on someone who reminded them of somebody back home?* She shrugged her shoulders and said in her mind, "*Well,*

———————— ∼ ————————

Melvin could feel beads of sweat popping out on his forehead as he dashed for the stairs. "Wow that was close!" He went out the first exit he saw. His heart was pounding so heavily he could hardly hear himself think. He had to go down a level to get to the Atrium, but at least from that point he could look around and find his way to the Purser's desk. He wasn't sure if that was where he wanted to go, but it was the best place he could think of to get information on how to change his assigned dining time. He was able to change his formal dining seating hour from 7:00 PM to 8:00 PM.

Since it seemed that Beverly wasn't going to be at her formal dinner seating tonight, Melvin decided to go back to his cabin. He didn't know why he was acting this way, because his plan was to approach Beverly. He had to ask himself what he was afraid of. Did he want to let her know how he felt, or didn't he? When he turned the corner, the corridors were lined with luggage. *'Great',* he thought; now I can shower and change before dinner. He showered and took a quick shave, and then he emptied his suitcase. He selected a short sleeve oxford shirt, and a pair of khakis to wear to dinner. He decided to empty his suitcase when he returned.

Melvin opened his cabin door, and peered up and down the corridor. He was hoping that Beverly's luggage was no longer sitting in front of her door. *Praise the Lord*! The two-piece paisley luggage set was no longer sitting in front of her cabin door. That meant she had gotten back to her cabin, and would probably be occupied for a while empting her suitcases. He breathed a sigh of relief knowing he would not run into her for the next hour or so, maybe even for the rest of the evening. Now, if he could figure out a decent way to let Beverly know that he was on board.

# Chapter 6

Brandon felt so much better. Not a trace of his previous seasickness lingered on. *Who knows… maybe he would run into that lovely angel of mercy, and get a chance to thank her?* Tommy had already hooked up with some young ladies who said they would meet him in one of the lounges some time before their dinner hour at 7:00 PM. Brandon made up his mind that if he was going to be on this cruise, he wasn't going to be ripping and running to every event and excursion that was offered.

Since this was his first cruise, he thought he would attend the meeting in the morning for the first-time cruisers. The meeting was to help them to get acquainted with the Do's and Do not's of cruising. The cruise director was also going to explain things like: carrying and exchanging currency, shopping on board and at ports, tours and excursions, unsafe ventures, and reliable transportation,

At dinner that evening their lead Server handed each person at the table menus and remove the folded linen napkin from their place settings; he draped it over their laps. That may have been a part of their professional training, but it made him feel kind of funny; so the next time around Brandon was going to beat him to the punch, and put his napkin across his own lap before the Server got to him.

Finally Thomas swaggered in. He took the vacant chair next to his father. Brandon surveyed the table. Most of the people seemed to be couples. He, Thomas, and an elderly gentleman appeared to be the only single ones at that table. There were two more empty seats, and during the course of the conversation, he found out that one of those seats belonged to the elderly gentleman's wife who was feeling a bit under the weather.

---

Beverly showered and thought she was going to put on a nightgown and relax for the rest of the evening. But that was crazy. That was the very thing she would do if she were still at home, *alone*. She grabbed the ships newsletter and checked the activities for the evening. Good! There was a Welcome aboard/Sail-a-way party on the open deck. She wasn't much for drinking and dancing, but she did want to hear the steel drum band. She kind of liked Calypso music and she especially wanted to see the colorful costumes the band would be wearing.

She put on a layered ruffle skirt, a colorful 'tee', her sandals. She picked up her sunglasses, and cross body purse from the dresser. Beverly took the elevator up two decks. She went down a short corridor, and through the heavy plastic car wash flaps that led out onto the Lido deck. The music was loud and lively. There were throngs of cruisers on deck laughing, dancing and having a great time.

Beverly looked at her watch. *Hum*, it was just about nine o'clock. She wasn't what one could say *hungry,* but a little something more to eat was an inviting thought. She went to the open dining area and put some crab salad and crackers on the plate. She dipped a medium-size portion of chocolate mousse in the desert bowl and placed it on the empty space next to her plate. On her way out, she stopped by the fountain area and got a Sprite adding a little amount of ice in the cup.

What luck! Just as she walked out on the deck, a couple was gathering their things to leave the table where they were sitting. Beverly asked them if they were coming back, and they said no. This was great. The table was close enough to the band, but distant enough so you weren't sitting on top of the speakers. Beverly was enjoying the atmosphere there. She was tapping her feet, and swaying in her seat. This was what they called the 'Sail-a-way party'. The band was singing "Olay, Olay-Hot, Hot, Hot'.

It's at times like this when something unexpected, something out of the blue happens. You're minding your own business, and *wham*! You're put on the spot. Every now and then some of the entertainers will call out over the microphone to a crew member, or a cruiser. Their voice would rise over the 'ting' of the steel kettle-drums in the same sing-song rhythm of the music to encourage activity. Beverly was being signal out. "Hey. Lady! You in the pretty skirt and the colorful blouse. I see you behind those sunshades. It looks like you want to dance. Stop *chair* dancing, and get out of your seat."

Beverly was turning her head looking from side to side to see who he was talking to. "Yes you he said in his heavy accent. Stop turning your head from side to side and come join in the fun." Beverly looked his way, and pointed to herself as if to say "*Who me*?" "Yes you, he said." She waved both hands in the air crisscrossing them back and forth to indicate *no*. Then, he said "We won't take *no* for an answer pretty lady. Somebody go get her, and bring her on the dance floor." Two men Tangoed their way over to her—a short, bald Caucasian guy in swimming trunks, and a middle aged man who could have been Hispanic. He was wearing a colorful floral print shirt and Bermuda shorts. They both took an arm and lifted her from her chair.

Beverly didn't want to dance with either one of them, but was relieved when the Hispanic man said,

"That's okay *Pops* I got this one." The other man Tangoed on, and the stranger danced her away from the table. Beverly raised her voice over the music to let him know that she hadn't danced in years, and he said that was all right because he could tell that she had not lost her rhythm.

Beverly wasn't that much out of touch with things that she couldn't recognize a come-on when she heard one. The mood of the dance was free-style and open, so she took a few steps and turns with him. The problem was that he kept trying to put his arm around her waist to draw her in closer to his body. She didn't mind the dance. It would have been a lot of fun if it wasn't for his obvious egotistical boldness. The music broke, and Beverly lifted her voice over the roar of the crowd.  "Thanks for the dance. It was fun", her tone indicating that it was the *one* and only dance he was getting out of her tonight.

She went back to her seat, discarded her food and kept her drink. Then, she walked by the fountain, refilled her cup, and added more ice. She went to the other side of the deck. She parted the sliding glass doors and stepped out into the moon light to enjoy the subtle ocean breezes. Finding a deck chair she sat down, breathed in deeply and smiled to herself thinking, *this is going to be a great vacation*!

———————~——————

Melvin felt more relaxed in knowing that Beverly had the early dining seating. Although the ship had two major formal dining rooms, he knew theirs was the same hour. He thought that if he could avoid her this evening, he would put a note under her door in the morning, or call her cabin to let her know that he was on board. He mauled it over and decided a call would be better than a note. Leaving a note under the door could make it look kind of sneaky like he was stalking her out or something; which in all actuality he had really done. At least with the phone call he could explain himself better.

Melvin showed the head maître d' his revised cruise pass, and he was directed to an area to the right side of the room. There weren't many people seated at the table, but it was still early. Melvin introduced himself saying this was his first cruise. Almost everyone at the table was a veteran cruiser, and they were full of suggestions and ideas for him. He peeked at his watch wondering when the waiters would begin to serve. Over his shoulder he could hear a group of ladies talking (a bit too loudly) for the quiet dining room setting, and they were headed straight towards his table. Melvin was floored when he saw that it was Anita, and some of her high school classmates.

Anita spotted Melvin at the table and a squeal of excitement escaped her lips. Melvin stood when they approached the table, and they rushed toward him in a fury of delight. Anita was saying "See I told you I saw him on board, now do you still think I'm crazy?" After the hugs and greetings were over they took their seats at the table. Of course, Anita grabbed the empty chair next to Melvin's, and the other two ladies grabbed whatever seating was left.

During the course of their chit-chat he found out that Anita was married (although she wasn't acting like it), and Betty was divorced. If he remembered liking any of the girls in the group, it was Betty. She was a very pretty, mannerly girl, and from what he could see, she maintained her figure and her looks very well. Vicky, on the other hand, was always the plain-Jane of the threesome. Well, to be honest, she was a bit on the 'homely' side. She was widowed when she was in her thirty's, and never remarried.

Melvin didn't know why silly thoughts popped into your head for no reason at all, and no matter how hard you try to forget thinking about them, they kept popping up. He glanced at Vicky a couple of times wondering how someone could look even homelier now than they did when you knew them years ago. Maybe the years hadn't been kind to her—at least they hadn't been kind to her face. She sure was one who didn't need to be in the sun for any length of time either. To him her teeth seemed more bucked than he remembered, and her *'froggy'* eyes were even more protruding.

It was awful, but he kept thinking…*Maybe her husband ran away from home*! It was stupid, but he couldn't get the vision out of his mind of someone packing up and taking off because they couldn't stand looking at ugly wife every morning. He tried to hold back a chuckle, but every now and then it slipped through. Other times he would smiled so hard that maybe he looked a little crazy to them. Hopefully they all thought that he was just enjoying the walk down memory lane. He could have kicked himself for secretly making fun at Vicky, but at least it took his mind off of Beverly for a little while.

The dinner was wonderful, and the service was excellent. Anita and Vicki invited him to go along with them and have a few drinks at one of the ship's bars, but he let them know that wasn't his style. He told them he wasn't much of a drinking man. Evidently, it wasn't Betty's style either. She begged off saying she was going to take an evening stroll around the deck, and then turn in for the night. That sounded good to Melvin too. Not that he wanted to go along with Betty.  The idea of a stroll around the ship sounded nice, but, he couldn't chance it. The ship had thousands of passengers; yet he almost crossed paths with Beverly earlier today. No, he would try and find a way to maneuver back to his cabin, hopefully without bumping into her.

# Chapter 7

Brandon knew he was a green horn when it came to cruising. This was his first experience and he already had a few unexpected surprises. He told Thomas he was going to attend the meeting for first-time cruisers that was being hosted by the ship's cruise director. But, his son said there was *no* way he was going to waste time sitting in a meeting with a bunch of nerds who needed instructions on how to have fun. He said he'd rather be out there doing it. They did agree to eat breakfast together at Breezes of the Sea. After all, he was the one who talked his dad into taking this Christmas cruise in the first place, so he couldn't completely abandoned him. They left for breakfast around 8:30 am, because the meeting was to start at 10:00 o'clock.

While they were eating Brandon looked at his tri-fold brochure, committing to memory the route to the ship's theatre where the meeting was to be held. Thomas told his dad he was going about things in the wrong way. He told him he would never meet anyone if he only followed a map around the ship all day. He said the thing to do was to *get* lost, or at least pretend you were lost, that way you could ask a pretty lady for directions. Brandon didn't respond to his son's suggestion, because in the first place, he never said he was taking the cruise to look for a lady friend. He smiled to himself when he envisioned Tommy running smack dab into a brawny, bodybuilding husband who was just turning the corner when Tommy was trying to lay a line on his wife.

~

Beverly sat near the middle of the spacious theatre on its main floor. The rear of the main level held horseshoe shaped, tufted booth lounges placed around tables for serving drinks. The second and third level balconies were set up in the same manner. Beverly was thankful for the additional information that was given in the meeting. It sort of took the edge off of her cruising along, and also helped her not to look so much like a first-time cruiser. She had not eaten much for breakfast, just a bagel with cream cheese, one sausage patty, some peaches and a cup of coffee. She was sure she would go to the Cafeteria to get some lunch, but first she wanted to walk around and take in the atmosphere.

The cruise director went over the scheduled activities for the day, and stated that passengers would receive a new itinerary either early every morning or late evening on a daily basis. Today was their day at sea, so there was plenty to do on board for the *savvy* cruiser. She was surprised to know that the photo gallery had already posted their boarding pictures, and last night's dinner pictures that were taken in the formal dining room. Beverly thought she would go up to the photo gallery to see if she could find her picture. She wasn't in the dining room last evening, so there was only one picture to look for. She hoped it didn't look hideous!

Beverly wasn't quite sure on how to go about finding her photo, there were so many of them, so she just started at the beginning of the rack. She stood admiring many of the photos, and wondered if she would bump into any of those people while cruising and remember their faces. There were other people looking through the racks as well, so she asked one of them if the photos were in any particular order. The lady explained that the beginning of the where she was standing posted everyone entering the ship during a certain time frame. The racks that were two sections down began the dinner seating photos from last evening. She said that by tomorrow afternoon the pictures from today's activities and this evening's dinner would be posted. Beverly thanked her and took a stroll over to the photo information desk to see if the cost of individual photos and packages was listed.

Melvin rang Beverly's cabin number for the second time. Maybe she had gone to breakfast and decided to take a stroll around the decks. He really wanted to phone her while she was in her cabin to let her know that he was on board. Although he knew this would still seem to have been dishonest and sneaky of him—at least it was better than just coming up on her unannounced. He wanted a chance to explain himself first. He didn't know if to involve Emily in it or not. Maybe he'd say he found out about her cruise from the family, and secretly booked the trip without their knowledge. Of course, then he'd have to tell her why. If he told her that, then what was he going to do with the story about the pre-class reunion?

Melvin thought about how he could have been having breakfast with Beverly or strolling with her around the deck. He even wanted to book an excursion or two, only he just didn't want to book it for himself. It was well after 11 o'clock and he wanted to eat lunch, but not in his cabin. Where was Beverly? Melvin decided to wait another half hour or so, and then try her cabin again. If that didn't work, he would just have to take a chance on leaving a handwritten note under her door.

Brandon came out of the meeting feeling a little more confidence about cruising. His thoughts ran to Grace, and he wished that they could have done something like this before she passed away. He wasn't so much grieved as he was perturbed. He could kick himself for not venturing out, not being more creative. But, if honesty counts for anything … he had been a penny pincher. He wasn't a miser, but they could have gone anywhere they wanted to go for free on Amtrak. It seems they never wanted to go anywhere much except to visit family. Most of the family still lived within driving distance of each other, but taking the train made it seem more like a vacation rather than a visit to a relative's house.

Brandon thought about when the boys were smaller. A couple of times that he reserved a sleeping car for the family. It wasn't a free ride like the coach seats were, but his employee discount gave him a great rate. The boys were so excited they hardly slept all night, and come to think of it, neither did he and Grace.
That fond memory bought a smile to Brandon's face.

He found himself kind of walking around not going anywhere in particular. He ended up on the level where the library and the photo gallery was. He remembered the cruise director mentioning something about the photos that were posted of them boarding the ship, so he veered off in that direction. There were several people standing at the extended hanging racks in the narrow corridor. The gallery also had pictures on the back walls of that section. He wasn't sure about way they were mounted, but most likely there was some kind of order. He reasoned that it probably was according to the times the passengers boarded the ship. He read through some of the information in his reservation packet and it said that although the ship had come in early that morning, it could not pull dock until after it had been inspected by the federal officers. Once the ship passed inspection, boarding could start any time after 1:00 pm, and the ship would pull dock promptly at 4:30 pm. He and Tommy boarded around three o'clock, so he started looking somewhere toward the middle of the rack for their photo.

# Chapter 8

Beverly walked back over to the photo wall to continue looking at pictures. Brandon looked up from glancing through a few racks to see Beverly standing at the next rack over. He was surprised that a ripple of excitement fluttered through his senses. Though normally a bit on the shy side (at least since he'd been widowed) he found himself making a bold step forward.

"Hello, there Florence Nightingale." Beverly looked over to see the man she had aided the day before. "Oh. Hello. How are you?" Brandon could tell his name slipped her mind. "Brandon; Brandon Woods, and I believe your name is… Beverly." He was surprised he remembered her name, and a little disturbed (though not *badly*) that she had not remembered his. They discovered they both had attended the first-time cruisers meeting. Beverly inquired as to how he was feeling today, and he said he was feeling much better.

Even though she had not gone to the formal dining room last night for dinner, she found out in the meeting that a lot of needed information for the cruisers was either printed, or electronically coded into their *ship-n-sail pass*. The dinner photos were posted under the heading of the dining room you were assigned to, and they were arranged under either the early or the late seating. Both she and Brandon had the early seating in the Flamingo Dining Room. Brandon said he would help Beverly to look for her boarding pictures. Again, he smiled at the thought of him remembering what she was wearing when she first came to his aid with the seasick pills.

Running her finger along the each photo, Beverly was dumbstruck when her finger landed on the photo of Melvin. Then, she wasn't *crazy!* She had seen him. Her face turned ashen, and the blood seemed to drain from the top of her head. Brandon was standing directly beside her and instantly noticed her pale appearance. He was in the midst of asking her what was wrong, when she appeared to become wobbly. He quickly stepped behind her and supported her back with his left arm at her waist, and he clutched her right elbow. "Whoa! You look at if you've just seen a ghost. Are you all right?"

Beverly couldn't speak. Her mind kept reeling around and around. Brandon decided to walk her over to the chair behind the information desk. Beverly's steps were heavy and staggered. What in the world! Brandon told her to sit in the chair and not to move; he was going to get some help. Beverly managed to speak before he moved from her side. "No. No, I'll be

Brandon didn't know what had just happened, but he felt his gentlemanly chivalry rise to the needed service. He offered to get Beverly a glass of water, but for some strange reason she didn't want this man; *this stranger* to leave her side. She asked him to stay with her for a moment and she was sure she would be okay. *Why would Melvin come on this cruise without letting me know? He wasn't anyone to be afraid of. He was a good family friend—yet this felt a little creepy.*

Brandon had crouched down beside Beverly's chair and was holding her hand. She must have been in somewhat of a daze because she never even realized he had sent a crew member for a glass of water. "Here, take a few sips of water, and then we're going to get you back to your cabin." He was still stooped at the side of her chair. He waited until Beverly took a few more sips out of the glass, and he handed it back to the crewmember. Brandon thanked the young gentleman for his service, and told him it looked like she was going to be all right.

He stood up and extended his hand toward Beverly. "Let's see your ship-n-sail card." Without any qualms or, hesitation Beverly reached into her little cross body bag and pulled out her card. "Umm", he said. You're just one level up from me, and almost directly over my cabin." He suggested taking the elevator because Beverly was still a bit wobbly on her feet. He supported her arm while they walked. When they got to her cabin, Brandon slipped the plastic card into the slot and pushed down on the handle. He gave the card back to Beverly and she stepped into her room. Feeling a little embarrassed, she thanked him again. Both of them said how odd it was that each of them had come to one another's rescue. Brandon looked down to see a note on the floor. "Hey" he said, it looks like someone left a note under your door." He stooped down to get the envelope from the floor and handed it to Beverly.

Brandon thought he wanted to invite Beverly to lunch, but it would have been rude to linger there since she was safely back in her cabin. Besides, he was a little rusty at asking a lady out. He was saying goodbye and was about to leave, when once again a pastiness gripped Beverly's face. But, this time because of what she read on the envelope. It was the same expression she had on her face up in the photo gallery. He didn't want to pry, but he had to ask if the note was from the same man whose photo she saw on the gallery wall. Her hands were trembling when she nodded her head *yes*.

"Are you in any sort of danger? Are you being stalked?"
"No, I don't think so, she said. This person is a longtime family friend. I don't know why I'm feeling this way about it, but I'm sure there's a reasonable explanation."

"Well, if you're sure you're going to be all right, I'll leave you to read your note. Look, if you should need me for anything I'll write my cabin number down for you, and you can give me a call."

Brandon reached for the unopened envelope and grabbed a pen from his shirt pocket. While he was writing the information on the notecard Beverly had a second thought. She really couldn't imagine what Melvin had written in the note, so just in case she needed some moral support, she asked Brandon to stay while she read it. He felt a little awkward about the whole thing, but he agreed to stay. The cabin door was left ajar and Beverly went to sit on the edge of the bed. She offered Brandon a seat at the small table, but he said he preferred to stand.

# Chapter 9

Brandon's eyes fell on the beautiful Christmas bouquet of flowers on the table in the corner. A tinge of jealousy entered his spirit, thinking that they might have been sent by the '*note writer*'.

"Well", Beverly said, "this note explains why Melvin is on board, and why he didn't get in touch with me before he left. He said he tried calling my cabin a couple of times since I've been on board, but never got an answer."
Without asking if he wanted to hear the personal information meant only for her, Beverly said, "Listen to this".

She told him the note said a little while back some classmates of his were planning a *non*-school reunion cruise just to get together. He told them he was not interested, but when he found out from my children that the cruise line and the dates were the same as mine, he scurried to get a ticket. He also said that as a family friend, he just wanted to be available. He got my cabin number from Emily and said he would let me know he was on board just in case I needed to look into a familiar face.

"I guess that explains everything, Brandon said, but why didn't he just asked you about it?"

"Oh, his note said he wanted to surprise me. Still, my spirit isn't quite certain that *all* has been said. I don't know why I feel so strangely about it."

Brandon felt his stomach rumble. He actually had intended to get lunch after he stopped by the photo gallery. "Well, I suppose you'll want to catch up with your friend, so I guess I'll be seeing you around." He opened the door wider to step into the corridor. Beverly got up and walked over to the door. "Say, I was going to get some lunch after I stopped by the photo gallery. Would you like to accompany me to lunch?"
Brandon was thrown for a loop. That's exactly what he had in mind, except he didn't know how to go about asking her. But, first he wanted to run by his cabin to freshen up and use the bathroom. He asked Beverly if he could pick her up in about twenty minutes. She said that sounded just fine.

———⁓———

When he saw Brandon leave Beverly's cabin, Melvin eased back into the room and closed the door. He had to take a few minutes to collect himself. *Who was this joker, and why did he have two help Beverly to her cabin in the first place? Was this some kind of a bootleg Casanova out to seduce women who traveled alone?*

Melvin was furious! Although legitimately; he had no right to be. He paced the floor several times trying to figure out what was going on. He reached for the phone, and then hung it up. He opened his cabin door to peek down at Beverly's cabin. The door was still on a crack. He shut his door again. He didn't know what to do. How did she know this man? Did she know him before her cruise? Was he a friend of hers that he didn't know about? This was crazy!

He could have been someone who just happened to help a lady in distress get back to her cabin. But, *"No"*, Melvin thought out loud. This character was invited in. Melvin saw when the man stooped down and picked up the note that he had written. *Not only that, but he stayed in there for another three or four minutes.*

Melvin didn't like the thought that maybe Bev had shared his personal note with a perfect stranger. He stopped pacing the floor and sat on the edge of the bed. He thought about the predicament he was in. He was a pretty *fair* Christian. He went to church. He admitted to himself that he wasn't a strong praying man. Maybe that's why he was sitting on a cruise ship, out in the middle of the ocean, at Christmas time thinking himself to be in *love* with his best friend's widow. And the kick in the head was, she probably never thought of him to be nothing more than her mechanic, and a family friend.

Now, Melvin felt a little silly. "At least", he said aloud, "I'm enough of a Christian not to sit here and pray that God would *make* Beverly *fall* in love with me. After all, she's never given me any indication that she thinks of me in that way. I guess I let my imagination get the best of me." He thought about how it was Ronald who walked him through some of the tough times when he was going through his divorce. *I was intrigued by how loving and precious his wife was, and wished that my wife could have been more like her. Yelp! This is entirely my fault.* Melvin knew his prayer life was weak. He didn't have a strong enough foundation to keep *flesh* from taking over his emotions. Yes, he admitted. I was definitely walking in a situation of *unrequited* love.

*No use trying to pull the wool over God's eyes now.* I've got to admit that I haven't been asking God about none of the plans He has laid out for my life. I've just been going along making my own plans, and making a lot of mistakes. Melvin thought about the lie he had written in his note to Beverly trying to explain why he was on the cruise. *What kind of way is that to begin a relationship, if there is to be one…starting out with a lie?*

Beverly freshened up her makeup, and pulled her hair back from her face. The whole idea of going to lunch with a man was foreign to her. Even more *bizarre*, was that they had just met yesterday. She nearly laughed out loud when she thought of what Emily would have said had she been there with her. Beverly heard a light tap on the door. She grabbed her sunglasses from the dresser and put them on. It wasn't that she would need them for any period of time; it's just that she needed something to hide her eyes so she wouldn't be caught staring at Mr. Woods.

When she opened the door Beverly came face-to-face with Melvin Blake. This was a person who was supposed to be a good family acquaintance. He was someone she frequently saw at church or saw when she took her car in to be serviced. So, why did she feel so indifferent about his presence now? Melvin was staring at Beverly like this was the first time he had ever laid eyes on her. It had been a while since he had stood this close to her. She was radiantly beautiful. Her skin was caramel brown and flawless. He couldn't look into her eyes, because the designer sunglasses she was wearing hid them—nonetheless to him, they made her even more mysterious and more alluring. Melvin was almost tongue-tied, but he had to say something. Anything was better than just standing there looking stupid.

"Hello Beverly, did you read my note?" Beverly's demeanor and attitude turned adverse. She said (very flatly) "Yes I got it, and I must say I'm still a little confused." Gazing down the corridor, Melvin could see the stranger that had been in Beverly's cabin headed their way. He had to talk fast. "Look, I would like to apologize for how this whole thing went down. To tell you the truth, I'm mighty embarrassed about it. Will you accept my apology?" He extended his hand as a token of friendship. "Friends", he said in a hopefully, questioning tone. Beverly extended her hand, and Melvin shook it as she said, "Okay, friends."

By that time Brandon reached the cabin door. Beverly introduced the gentleman, and they greeted each other; *a bit on the cool side by Melvin*, with a handshake. Brandon didn't want to prolong the time, so he turned his attention to Beverly and said, "Shall we go?" Beverly closed her cabin door, and Brandon gave a nod of his head toward Melvin saying, "Nice to have met you." They turned to leave, and Beverly said "Well, I guess I'll be seeing you around the ship. Oh, by the way if you didn't realize it already, your picture is posted up in the photo gallery. I was shocked when I saw that you were on this ship." With that said, Melvin realized he was losing ground, and along with it; maybe his chance with Beverly.

# Chapter 10

Betty had been called a *'party pooper'* before, so she didn't mind (much) when Anita threw the title on her again. To be a married woman, Anita was just *too* loud and flirting for Betty's liking. She'd always been sort of *out there,* but some of the things she did on this cruise were down right embarrassing. Now, she was going to go up to the purser's desk to sign everyone up for tomorrow's shore excursion. And, of course Vicki was her tag-a-long shadow no matter what she wanted to do.

Betty made the excuse that since this was her first time cruising she wanted to explore the ship a little more. She told Anita to count her out, saying she would probably sign up for the Spa package instead. What she really didn't want to do was to go ashore with Anita and Vicki not knowing what to expect; especially since she knew Anita was only booking the excursion because of the man she met last night in the Piano Lounge. He and his friend said they had gone on the excursion the last time they cruised with this ship, and they wanted to see if the tour was the same at

Christmastime. They said it was a great tour, and maybe Anita should come along too.

———————～———————

The threesome stayed longer than they had expected at lunch. They kept going back sampling foods they had never tried before, and ended up close to the point of gluttony. After lunch Anita and Vicky left to book their excursion. Betty decided to take a stroll around the ship. She ended up checking out the Spa. She wasn't interested in the facials, although the body massages were reasonable. The sauna and whirlpool caught her attention too. Maybe that was because they were free. She wasn't a cheapskate, but she had never cruised before, and since this was such a long cruise, she wasn't sure what monies she would need for later on. Betty figured she would put the Spa on her list of things to do for tomorrow while the other girls were touring the island. For now, she was going back to the cabin to get the book she brought with her. It was an interesting novel and she wanted to read a couple more chapters.

Betty knew her girlfriends laughed at her behind her back, but at least she was honest with herself—even though she was a *'hopeless'* romantic, she didn't fall in love with every guy she met. Betty thought about Anita's marital situation. She didn't know any personal information, but she was sure it wasn't all peaches and cream. A red flag went up when she heard Anita say, "He's so boring, I can't *do* church all the time." Betty was secretly praying for an opportunity to sit alone with her schoolmate so they could talk. She wasn't trying to pry into her private affairs, but she could sense that Anita was running from something, and trying to cover it up with nightclubbing and care-free fun was not going to solve her problem. Betty prayed that the Lord would give her Godly advice, and encouraging words to share with her friend.

---

Brandon and Beverly were unsure how to go about sitting as a twosome for lunch. They didn't know if to find a table first, and then allow one of them go to get their food while the other waited at the table, or should they both fill their plates, and walk together to find a table? They were standing in the entryway of the dining area putting these questions to each other, and had to laugh at their humorous dilemma. *More than likely, they probably were laughing at themselves for being single so long they didn't even know how to sit with a stranger.* Brandon suggested they get their soft drinks, silverware, and napkins. Then he would carry everything over to a table.

He chose a table that would give them a view of the beautiful ocean waters. The calm blue waves rippled across the surface with the effortless movement of the huge cruising vessel. When he saw Betty gawking through the crowd looking for him, Brandon stood to wave his hand in the air to get her attention. It was a good thing too, because just that quickly the scenario with Melvin flashed in her mind, and she forgot whose face she was looking for.

Brandon held Beverly's chair out for her when she got to the table. *"Hum, she thought, he's a real gentleman."* It had been a long time since a gentlemen held her chair out for her. Brandon felt a mixture of chivalry and awkwardness. The last time he sat alone with a woman it was his wife. He hoped his nervousness didn't show. Gathering up his courage, he moved from behind Beverly's chair to take the seat across from her. He purposely deepened his voice to hide any nervous pitch that might have crept in, and said, "How 'bout we bless the food first, and that way you won't have to wait for me to return with my plate?"

Beverly bowed her head and waited for him to offer the blessing. It was short, but she could tell it was not a put on. When he opened his eyes, he saw a smile on Beverly's face.  It must have been one of approval because she simply said, *"thank you"*. Brandon rose from his seat saying he would be right back.  He was somewhat proud of his accomplishment, and could have almost strutted like a peacock—but he didn't!

The two of them shared a little about each of their previous marriages, and some of their present singleness.  They shared how they came to be on this particular cruise (each by different circumstances). The conversation was light and friendly, although at one time or another each of them thought silently of their deceased spouses.

It was refreshing to hear the faint holiday accompaniment in the background. Most of it was instrumental, and could be heard throughout the ship continually during the day. Brandon was surprised how much he and Beverly both loved the Christmas season and why it was so strange for them to be away from family at this time of year.

Beverly talked about what she probably would be doing if she were at home right now, and she was very much surprised when Brandon told her he would be baking several varieties of Christmas cookies. He admitted he wasn't a great cook. He said that it was one of the family traditions he and his late wife used to do, and he tried to continue some of them, because it brought back joyous memories.

Beverly said since it was December 23rd, most likely this evening she would have been  anxiously waiting to sit in front of the TV and watch either 'SCROOGE', or 'IT'S A WONDERFUL LIFE'. Brandon got a kick out of that because he said that's exactly what he would be doing too.

They began to share with each other some of their family traditions and other favorite holiday things, and before they knew it; what they thought would have been a casual hour or so lunch between two people who just met, slipped into a two hour connection between friends.


Beverly was thinking, *"This is crazy. You didn't come on this cruise to act like a silly high school girl, or to have a fling with a complete stranger."* Yet, Brandon didn't feel like a complete stranger. This was their third encounter, and as much as she wanted to convince herself that she was okay with her aloneness; denial wouldn't help her to minimize the fact that she actually had begun to take interest in this man. *A perfect stranger! A man she just met yesterday of all things!*

As they were leaving the Breezes of the Sea, Brandon thanked Beverly for having lunch with him.  They had made such a connection, and shared so much of their life stories with each other; he couldn't just leave it at; '*Well I guess I'll be seeing you around*'. He remembered from looking at her Pass-Card that she had the early seating for dinner. Maybe that would be his opportunity to see her again. Then something came to mind. It was something she said during lunch.

"Hey Beverly, I know a way we can be on this cruise, and not break with one of our Christmas traditions.  After dinner tonight may I escort you to the Palace Theatre?" Beverly wasn't sure what an extended outing with this man had to do with their family traditions. "*So*... tell me what does that have to do with one of your, or my family tradition?" Brandon was already fishing in his back pant pocket for the folded newsletter for the day. He unfolded it, leaned in closer to Beverly, and scrolled his finger down on one side until it came to rest on a certain item. He bent down a little and said, "Feast your eyes on this." Beverly said, "Are you kidding me? Scrooge! The Broadway show for tonight is *Scrooge?*" She almost squealed in delight. Brandon said, "Well, is it a date?" Even after he said it, he couldn't believe he had asked her. But, without any hesitation, Beverly said '*yes*'.

Beverly had to admit she was enjoying Brandon's company and wanted it to last a little while longer. But how could she go about it? Lunch was over, and he was sure to leave and go do whatever his plans might have been for the rest of the afternoon. Suddenly an idea popped into her head. When he came to her rescue earlier today she was in the photo gallery looking for her picture, so she took in a deep breath and asked him if he wouldn't mind going back to the gallery to look for their pictures.

While they were picking out photos, Brandon asked Beverly what her plans were for tomorrow. She said she didn't have any definite plans, other than to hang around the ship, go to the Spa and to browse through some of the on-board shops. Now it was Brandon's turn to take a *leap of faith* and ask if she wanted to go ashore with him when they docked at St. Thomas. Brandon pushed past his generally timid nature to pose the question, and she said 'yes' again. After coming from the photo gallery, he walked her back to her cabin, and standing at the door, gave her hand a gentle squeeze saying, "Thank you for the day, and I guess I'll meet you after dinner." He had no idea that the vacant seat at his table belonged to Beverly Sparks.

# Chapter 11

Melvin sensed the offense in Beverly's voice when she hinted at his underhandedness. He still didn't get a chance to explain anything to her. If only he had a few more minutes before that *'but-in-ski'* Brandon showed up. He wanted to explain what really happened. But, now he didn't have that chance. Melvin thought about the lie he had already written in the note, and wondered how he could work around that. Things had gotten a little out of hand. Now, he was glad he had changed his dining hour to the second seating—at least that way he had less of a chance bumping into Beverly. She would most likely be cordial, but that was probably all he could expect.

He had to clear his thoughts. He decided to get some fresh air. He left his cabin thinking, *'at least if I run into Bev now, it won't be such a shock to her.'*

He cut across the Atrium and took the stairs up to the next level. When Melvin started out, he was headed for the outer decks, but all of a sudden changed directions mid-course, and headed for the library. He wasn't sure why, but maybe it was just to sit alone in solace. Of course that didn't make any sense to him because he'd just left his cabin where he had been sitting alone in solace. Well—at least he had been sitting; maybe more in *repentance* than in solace.

Betty sat in the library reading the novel she brought with her. She started reading *'Pastor Q and Donna' (A Christmas Surprise)* last week, but didn't finish it because there was so much to do to get ready for the cruise. She tucked the book in her carry-on bag intending to read some more of it on the flight, but that didn't work either.  Her friends *blabbed* away the whole time, and before she knew it the plane was coming in for a landing. The book was a romance novel about a pastor and his wife, and the many things they shared together during the Christmas season. Betty loved Christmas. This would be her first experience away from her immediate family, *and of all things*, she was celebrating the holiday on a cruise ship. She was happy to know that along with the other *gayeties* of the season, there would be a traditional Christmas service held in the chapel on Christmas morning.

Betty looked up from her book when she heard the library door open.  She saw Melvin before he saw her, and for a quick instant she wanted to turn her back, or cover her face with her book, but thought the additional movement would bring attention to her even more.

Melvin didn't know why he had detoured off into the library.  So, just for the sake that he had ventured in there, he decided to take a quick look around. Betty had only a moment to turn her face back down to her reading, but it wasn't quick enough for Melvin not to notice her.  A wave of unexpected pleasure swooped through his thoughts, and he closed the library door behind him.  He moved slowly toward the table where Betty was sitting. She kept her eyes plastered on the page she wasn't really reading knowing that he was headed in her direction. She didn't know why, but she felt butterflies in her stomach, and a slight clamminess in the palm of her hands.

"Well, fancy meeting you here."  Betty looked up straight into Melvin's very kind, but somewhat troubled looking brown eyes.  All she could manage to say was "Hi."  When another patronage of the library passed by their table Melvin lowered his voice. "Mind if I join you?" Betty extended her hand to indicate the empty chair across from her and said, "No I don't mind. Have a seat." Melvin asked what she was reading, and she was almost too embarrassed to say it out loud, so instead she lifted the book from the table facing the cover toward him so he could read the title. "*Hum that* sounds interesting. Anybody you know?" Betty looked over the top of the book at Melvin. She had a questioning look on her face, and then she noticed the smile creeping up on his face. He was just joking.

Melvin wanted to know where the rest of the *gang* was; so she went into the explanation of them purchasing tickets for their shore excursion tomorrow. Betty said she didn't sign up with them because she was pretty sure they were going to venture off the beaten path to places unknown, and she didn't want to be tagging along like a *third* wheel. What she really was thinking was—she didn't want to end up lost on an Island where she'd never been before, or chance getting back too late; *missing the boat.*

Melvin told her he had originally planned to go on shore, but his plans were unexpectedly interrupted (he was thinking of Beverly).  Betty noticed that when he made that statement, a sudden sadness shadowed his demeanor. She was tempted to ask if anything was wrong, but pushed the thought out of her mind.  She had to get out of the habit of trying to fix everyone's problems, and start concentrating on '*Betty*'.

It looked like she wasn't going to get much more of her reading in, not that she minded, so she gently closed her book. Melvin said he was on his way to the photo gallery when he stopped in the library. He asked Betty if she wanted to go along with him, and she said *she didn't mind.*

———————⁓———————

Brandon offered to pay for Beverly's photo, but she turned him down. When he found the photo of his dining table group, Beverly realized they were assigned to the same dining room, but she didn't tell him that. *Good,* she thought, *that will make it easier for us to meet up after dinner for the stage show.* After their purchases both of them went back to their cabins to relax before their dinner hour. Beverly really wanted to freshen up and change into something less casual for the evening.

Tommy was in the cabin when his dad got back. He asked where he had been all this time. Brandon could see that Tommy was worried about him. He told his dad he was just about to call security. He tried to say it in a jokingly way, but Brandon could tell that his son was serious about it. Tommy was thrown for a loop when his dad told him about his escapade.

He couldn't believe that his father had met a lady yesterday who had come to his rescue. They had already gone to lunch together, and now they were going to the theatre together this evening.

"Wow! Looks like my technique of meeting ladies isn't working for me. Maybe I'd better try doing whatever it is that you're doing! I guess I'd better start *'rolling'* with the *'Big boys'*, or at least change some of my moves." "That's just it son. This wasn't about me making '*a move*', or having a technique. It was just…well, just about two people meeting under unusual circumstances. It wasn't plotted, or planned—at least not by me." "Okay Pops", Tommy said, "I get it. So, when am I going to meet this lady?" Brandon told Tommy he wasn't sure. He only knew they both had the early seating for dinner, and that he and Beverly were going to wait for each other near the railing facing the dining room after dinner.

～

Anita and Vicky were more than a little curious about Betty's delinquent return to the cabin. They started right in giving her the *third degree* hoping to prod information out of her on where she had been. She didn't lie to them. She just didn't tell them the whole truth; after all, what she did was her own business—at least for now. She told them she had gone to the library to read, and after that she went one level up to the photo gallery. Betty reached between some pages in her novel and pulled out her photos to share with her friends. Vicky and Anita were so excited about going to search for their pictures; they dashed out of the cabin without asking another word about her venture. Closing the door behind them Betty chuckled to herself. Then she felt badly about what she was thinking, because she had seen their pictures, and for what it was worth—neither one of them needed to be breaking their necks getting to the photo gallery.

Betty was glad she had some time to herself. This time she wasn't trying to catch up on her reading. She had a bigger dilemma to think about. It was nice walking to the photo gallery with Melvin. She took note of the way people looked at them, as if they were a couple. Their conversation was a bit awkward, but nice just the same. He asked her about old school chums; of which she was little help. She had to admit she didn't keep up with the *how,* and *what* in the lives of the other people in their graduating class. If Melvin wanted to know that, all he had to do was to ask Anita. She was the walking encyclopedia of gossip. She knew more about everybody's life than she knew about her own. That became evident when she and her husband almost got a divorce. Her marriage was still on the brinks, and she wasn't helping things any.

Betty's slight reminiscing caused her to divert from the situation at hand. What was going to happen tonight when she and Melvin were seated at the same table for dinner? How would she act, or better still… *react?* She would be so embarrassed if her friends noticed anything different between her and Melvin tonight that wasn't going on between them last night.

After they had selected their pictures, she and Melvin walked by the open self-service area on the upper deck to get a soft serve ice cream cone. Betty remembered saying something to the effect of not wanting to splurge too much before dinner, and Melvin made a comment about her attractive *'high-school'* figure; saying how pleasing it was to see that some women maintained themselves *very* nicely. His glance moved quickly from her face all the way down to her calves, and then rising, focused on her face again.  She remembered blushing. It wasn't just what he said, it was the way he said it. The reminder caused her to blush again just thinking about it. They parted at the elevator. Melvin thanked her again for her company, and said what a pleasure it would be to see her again tonight at dinner.

# Chapter 12

Emily cringed every time she thought about the short message Melvin left on her cell phone before he sailed. Now, instead of feeling confident that her mother was being guarded by a close family friend, her Mom could end up being stalked by a man who horded secret feeling for her; and *she* was the cause of it all.

Emily's husband could tell that something was bothering her. She was usually upbeat and excited about the holiday season, but for the last couple of days she seemed to have been edgy and short-tempered with everyone. Wayne thought that something may have gone wrong at the Day Care center. But, when he talked to his wife about his concerns, he was glad that everything was going well at work. However, he just about *'blew'* his top when he found out that she had been meddling in her mother's affairs. He sympathized that after her father passed away, Emily took it upon herself to feel responsible for the care of the family— even though most of them were of age. The youngest was Carol who was just about to enter the 9th grade, and her brother had already graduated high school. Emily just didn't understand that her overly protective nature soon became an unconscious habit of trying to control other people's lives. The *double* Christmas celebration thing was a good idea, but it ruined their budget. Since the schools were closed, and some of the Day Care centers had limited hours for the holidays, Wayne thought this would give him the opportunity he needed to spend more time with his wife discussing a few things she needed to deal with.

———～———

Brandon was floored, but pleasantly surprised when he looked up to see Beverly being directed by one of the Servers to the table where he was sitting. Tommy took note of the expression on his dad's face. '*Soo*', he thought. '*Could this be the lady in question?*' The Server pulled the empty chair out for Beverly that was directly across from where Brandon was sitting. When she was seated and scooted her chair closer to the table, the Server gracefully laid the half folded napkin across her lap and handed her the large burgundy folder that housed the dinner menu. It was only when she lowered her menu that Beverly realized she was sitting directly across the table from the man who had been on her mind for the last two hours…Brandon. Brandon Woods. A small gasp escaped through her parted lips, but a pleasant smile crowned her face.

Beverly cleared her throat, and began introducing herself around the table. The response to her introductions started at her left, and circled around the table. Thomas detected a certain gleam in his father's eye when it came to his introduction. *"Ah-ha"*, he thought, also introducing himself to Beverly; *now I'm sure this is the elusive stranger he met on board yesterday.* Brandon searched his menu trying to make a decision before the Server got around to him. He knew he was hungry, but the thought of food went clean out of his head when Beverly sat down across from him. *What's the matter with me? I feel as awkward and clumsy as a shy school boy.* He was afraid that if he'd try to speak, his words would either stammer out, or be two octaves higher than usual.

Brandon felt a poke on the arm. Tommy had nudged him with his elbow. Evidently this was the second time he had asked him what he was going to order. He steadied his voice and told Tommy he wasn't sure, he was still looking. Tommy leaned over to whisper in his dad's ear. "Yeah, you sure were looking, but it wasn't at the menu." He had to admit, his son was right. He could only hope he wasn't that conspicuous to everyone else. Beverly was very *eye* catching, but not overly done. She had stepped up from the casual attire she had on earlier this afternoon to a dressier look. It wasn't formal or anything like that. It was sort of dressy-casual. Brandon didn't know how to phrase it. It was nice. Yes…very nice.

This was the second night out, and the dining room was serving lobster. There were other mouth-watering things on the menu as well, but Brandon said to himself; *'Well since they went through all the trouble of catching so many lobsters, he might as well accommodate the chef and eat a couple of them.'* A lobster dinner and a theatre date with a beautiful lady; it didn't get much better than that!

———— ～ ————

Anita and Vicky returned to the cabin complaining about the way their pictures turned out. Of course they blamed everything and everyone from the lighting to the photographer for their less than perfect photos.  What she had to ask herself was, why did they pay good money for something they weren't satisfied with? Maybe it was just to prove when they got back home, they had been on a cruise.

Before Anita and Vicky had come back to the room, Betty tried her best to remember Melvin from high school.  She remembered he was in a couple of her classes, and he played football.  He was also on the Debate team, and was in the Science Club (strictly for *brainy-acts*). He was in a lot of school activities, but wasn't much for socializing when he was not there. He was definitely not the *parting* type. But, being a bit of an introvert herself, she didn't keep up with the in-crowd.

He was kind of *'buff'*, and now that she thought about it, he did try to talk to her a few times. She remembered how shy she was, and when guys spoke to her, she couldn't get past a quick '*hello*' before she ran in the opposite direction. It was all coming back to her now. He was the one who invited her to his eighteenth birthday party. He passed the invitation to her when she was leaving class. Of course she didn't go. After that, she heard he was dating some girl on the cheerleading squad. They ended up getting married half way through college.

Anita and Vicky were yammering on about something, but Betty wasn't paying much attention to them.  As usual, they were talking about some guy they met, or wanted to meet. While they yapped on, Betty had second thoughts about going to dinner.  She didn't want to skip dinner altogether, just the formal seating in the Flamingo Dining room. Actually, it was sitting at the table with Melvin that bothered her.  Oh, he seemed nice enough, and he certainly was a gentleman, but she wasn't sure if his friendliness toward her would lead to something she wasn't quite prepared for.

Romantic interludes and intimate settings are the business of cruise ships, and if one isn't careful, she or he could get caught up in the illusion of its fantasy. Things could move along very rapidly when you're on a floating vessel that toots all the right horns and blows all the right whistles; but when you get back home to reality…things could appear to look differently.

*No*. She had to slow down and think for a minute. She needed more time by herself in order to clear her head. They had the late seating for dinner, nonetheless she thought about skipping it. But, what if Melvin was looking forward to seeing her? Betty thought to herself, *I'm on a cruise ship with hundreds of people, and I feel one of my 'I want to be alone moments' coming on me.* She ended up telling her friends to go along with whatever plans they had for now, and she would catch up with them later on. Betty knew she was stretching the truth, but she didn't want to have to explain herself to them if she told the whole truth.

---

Brandon waited for Beverly in the hallway near the theatre while she used the power room.  He fished in his front pant pocket for a breath mint, and popped it in his mouth. He was as nervous as a cat in a dog pound. Things kept running through his mind like; *should I hold her arm as we walk together in the theatre? Should I stand on her right side or her left? Should we walk together to the entryway, and then I take the lead and let her follow me down the aisle?* The most popular saying going around the church was: "What would Jesus do?" Brandon had to laugh at himself when he tried to imagine Jesus escorting a lady into a theatre to see 'Scrooge'.

This scenario is certainly one that that question couldn't answer. How could he have felt so comfortable with this woman one minute, and be a bundle of nerves the next? Just when the urge to dash to the restroom came upon him, Beverly was walking his way. *"Well, he thought, I'll just have to excuse myself to the men's room after we get seated."*

Beverly felt a little more confident when she emerged from the lady's room, but she was still nervous. This was stepping outside of her *motherly* roll— as nurturer. This wasn't coming to someone's aid, or bumping into them again and deciding to have lunch together. This was an actual date! The realization of the situation overwhelmed her when they left the dining room, and she escaped to the nearest lady's room before her legs wobbled out from under her. She had to catch her breath and clear her thoughts. She had been so many things to so many people, she didn't know how to be herself. Where was the real Beverly? Did she know how to be her? Isn't that why she come on this Christmas cruise—to do something for her? While touching up her makeup and applying fresh lipstick, she was silently praying about taking the first step of this new adventure. That's when she heard the voice of her youngest daughter in her head. Carol was saying… *'remember Mom, Old School, or New School, it doesn't matter. Chivalry is not dead. Men still need to take the lead.* Carol was single. She was wise. Beverly thought…she is *me!*

Brandon was standing near the open theatre doors. "Well there you are. I thought I'd lost you", he said. Beverly thought to herself…*You don't know how close you are to the truth.* She smiled as she stood facing him.  The fragrant aroma of her perfume reached his nostrils. It was a familiar fragrance, and it caused him to feel even more relaxed and at ease. Beverly spoke first. "I think I'd better follow you." "But, I don't know where I'm going either', he said. "That's all right, I'm sure with your height you can spot some good seats for us better than I could." She stepped slightly behind him placing her hand midway the back of his sports jacket. With that, Brandon pressed forward with all the confidence he could muster up—feeling like a Trojan horse knocking down the walls of Troy.

# Chapter 13

Vicky already had reservations about the men she and Anita had promised to meet. They were supposed to meet in the Calypso Lounge before dinner. She knew that as plain looking as she was, she didn't stand a chance of attracting any men on her own, so she hung with Anita. She began doing that way back when they were in high school. She met her husband Thaddeus because of hanging with Anita. Thaddeus was coming out of a *Love Affair* gone sour, and Anita convinced him to join her and some friends at the club that Friday night. She was the only one in their crowd who was still single. The two of them got together. And although she knew Thad married her on the *'rebound'*, she tried to make it last for as long as she could.

Vicky knew she was going to end up going with Anita but, was a little uneasy on several levels.  She didn't trust Anita's judgement, the cute guy was already *'high'* when they met him that afternoon, and the only other person she had faith in decided not to hang with them.  The one thing she knew about herself was that she may not be the most attractive woman in the world, but she was alive, had good sense, owned her own house and car, and was not about to give some *Gigalo* all her money for a roll in the hay. Vicky thought to herself: *I may be a little desperate…but I'm not stupid!*

What she really wanted to do was to go to see 'Scrooge' at the theatre, but Anita said; "Girl, with all this *'fresh game'* on board I'm not about to sit in an auditorium watching some lame, boring stage play." Vicky knew that if she had enough courage to make her own choices, she would've try and hang with Betty, but Betty seemed to be off doing her own thing. If the cruise had only been a little later, she would have been able to pay the full amount on her own. But, Anita told her not to worry about it, she would put the rest of the balance on her credit card, and she could pay her back when they got home.

———～———

Beverly was enjoying the play. It ended up being more of a musical rather than a Drama; for which she was glad. She and Brandon knew the story well it made them chuckle when they said the next line right along with the actors. Beverly's mind floated back to her family several times, but she didn't let it linger there. What really got her was that she didn't feel as guilty as she thought she would feel by being away from them.  Maybe it was because the Lord had caused her to meet Brandon on her first day aboard, and he didn't feel like a stranger when she spoke with him. He may not be *'the One'*, but she had to admit, it was odd the way they met.

What was scarier still, was that she wasn't afraid to approach him. She felt comfortable being around him; just like it was with Melvin. *Oh boy!* Why did she have to think of that incident? A flux of anger began to well up in her spirit, when all of a sudden she felt the touch of a warm hand on her arm. She heard a man's voice gently whisper her name. It gave her a slight *start.* It was Brandon asking if everything was alright.

Beverly told him everything was great, and he asked if she wanted some refreshments. There was going to be a brief intermission, and the waiters were moving through the audience to see about refilling the orders of alcoholic beverages, or whatever people were drinking.  She said no, she was just fine. *But she wasn't.* Now, she was a little embarrassed wondering how long she had been unresponsive to his prodding during her musing. Beverly didn't want him to think she was bored, or anything like that, because she wasn't. As a matter of fact she felt just the opposite. Brandon was very suave, although he didn't know it. At least she sensed he didn't think that of himself. He excused himself to use the men's room. A special guest artist came on stage to sing Christmas carols with the audience. Beverly guessed the crew was back stage changing the scenery for the second act.

It's amazing the illusions that can be produced today through electronic light projection and images. Everything seemed so beautiful, so magical. I'm glad Brandon came back in time to

enjoy the singing before it was all over. The soloist
had a beautiful voice, and I was delighted that she
sang a good mixture of sacred along with the
secular Christmas carols. Every now and then she'd
lower my voice to listen to Brandon sing. Beverly
was pleasantly surprised. The man could *Sing*!

After the show, Brandon asked if Beverly
wanted to go for coffee and dessert. Having the
early dinner seating left time to get involved in
several on board evening activities, but it also left
one desiring a little snack before bedtime. He
suggested going back to 'Breezes of the Sea' where
they had gone for lunch. She was glad for that
because it was an open atmosphere and a very
public place. Going to one of the lounges would
have been a might too *cozy* for our two-day
acquaintance.

They sat at a booth where they could view
the open sea. Beverly thanked him for the evening,
and commented on his lovely singing voice. He
chuckled giving an elusive, but subtle smile. He
told me he even surprised himself; because he had
not sung in a long time. He took a sip from his
coffee cup, and still holding it at face level, peered
over the rim and said, "Maybe it's the atmosphere
and the lovely company that kindled the moment."
Beverly was so dazzled by the statement, that she
felt a little self-conscious. It had been so long since
she had received a (somewhat *flirty*), but flattering

compliment from a gentleman, she could barely whisper out her "Thank you".

Beverly was enjoying herself, but this was so out of the norm for her. She was kind of an early bird about getting to bed. If she were at home, she would have been preparing for bed hours ago. However, she wasn't at home. She was on a cruise ship. She was sitting across the table from a handsome gentleman, and having a wonderful evening.

They both were on their second rounds of coffee and dessert. It must have been later than they thought, because Brandon suddenly looked down at his watch. The ships servers and waiters were clearing the food from the buffet stations, and washing down the equipment. "Wow, do you know what time it is?" Then he answered his own question before Beverly could say anything. "It's past midnight." "What!" Beverly was just as surprised as he was. "Where did the time go?"

Brandon knew he didn't have any solid plans for tomorrow—at least he didn't when he got on board yesterday, but now that he'd met Beverly, a morning in St. Thomas seemed very pleasing. Originally he told his son he would go along on the cruise, but don't expect him to go following around behind him like a puppy dog. *'Well'*, he guessed no truer worlds had ever been spoken, because they really hadn't seen that much of each other since the first day of the cruise.

He asked Beverly if she had any plans for tomorrow, and she told him 'no'; no more than to hang around the ship, and maybe go to the spa. Brandon thought it was probably too late to buy an excursion ticket for in the morning, but he knew he wanted to spend more time with this lovely lady. He may have been going out on a limb, but he didn't feel that she would turn him down if he asked her to go ashore for a walk, or maybe a short taxi ride around the island. Beverly said *"Yes. No use coming this far and not stepping foot on the Virgin Islands."* Brandon said that was his exact same thought. They agreed to meet near the glass elevator in the *Atrium* at 1:00pm. That way each of them could have their own morning time, and there wouldn't be throngs of people crowding the elevators and corridors exiting for their planned excursions.

---

Melvin tried not to let his face show his disappointment when only Vicky and Anita showed up for the dinner seating. He thought he and Betty had clicked on a few levels, and was surprised when she didn't show for dinner. Was everything okay? Was she feeling ill? Did he come on too strong and scare her off? *Maybe,* he thought, *I was so wrapped up in my own male ego, and embarrassment with the way things turned out with Beverly, I rebounded too fast onto Betty hoping to recovery my feelings.* So many questions ran through Melvin's mind, he didn't know what to think.

He didn't want to draw any suspicion to himself, or for that matter to Betty, so when the moment was right, and they were waiting for the main entrée, he nonchalantly said, "So, where is your friend tonight? He purposely omitted saying her name. Does she have a 'hot' date?" Anita laughed out loud, as if that were an impossible thing for her friend. "Oh please, are you kidding?" Then she said something about Betty saying she had something to do, and she would meet them at dinner if she didn't get detained. Melvin didn't like the sarcasm in Anita's remark, and inwardly wanted to come to Betty's defense. But, he felt himself jumping the gun again, and didn't want to do more harm than good, so he swallowed the urge, and took another drink from his water glass.

Melvin joined in the conversation as much as possible, and tried not to look conspicuous every time a slender 'black' woman entered in the dining room and appeared to be headed in their direction. Inadvertently, the new comer would veer off in another direction to find her own awaiting friends. His mind was not on his meal. It was on Betty. If it wasn't for the fact that she had already shared with him how the three of them happened to be sharing the same cabin; he would still be wondering how three women so unlike each other could be on a cruise together.

Melvin came out of his absorbed thoughts to find Vicky smiling at him. He wasn't sure if he had missed something amusingly said at the table, or worse yet; in not hearing her, did he agree with something she just said? Lucky for him, she repeated her question. "You know you can send your steak back if it's not done to your liking, don't you?" It was evident that those at the table were moving along with their meals while his plate had hardly been touched.

"Oh no", he replied. It's really delicious; I guess I'm not as hungry as I thought. It must be all those in-between meals I've helped myself to today." His comment about all the food available on the cruise started a whole new conversation around the table; which was just the diversion he needed. He did have a longing…*a hunger* if you will, and that was to see Betty again. *It's kind of funny,* he thought. *I haven't thought of Beverly all day, and she's the reason why I came on this cruise in the first place…or was it?*

# Chapter 14

Beverly went through the preliminaries of preparing for bed, however, she knew she would not fall asleep—at least not right away. She was far too excited. When she and Brandon left Breezes of the Sea, she really would have liked to have taken a stroll around the deck, but with the moonlight, the music, and the allure of romance in the air, she could almost bet it would have led to a romantic good night kiss. She could sense it in her spirit, and that's exactly why she didn't want Brandon to walk her back to her cabin. She couldn't guess what his feelings were, but she knew what was welling up inside her; and her feelings were racing just a little too quickly for her. It had been almost five years since Ronald passed away, and any little old thing could stir her emotions.

She couldn't believe God's timing. Just the excuse she needed showed up at the elevator at the same time she and Brandon awaited its ascent. It was Tommy! Evidently coming from a moonlight escapade of his own, he was shocked to find his dad standing at the elevator. Tommy was speechless. When the elevator arrived, they all stepped in together. Beverly quickly taking advantage of the situation said, "Why don't you two gentleman continue on together. I can see myself to my cabin."

Before Brandon could respond, she bade him goodnight, thanking him again for a wonderful evening, and quickly stepped from the elevator before the doors closed.

～

Betty could not have been more miserable if she had planned it. This is crazy! Betty thought the time she wanted to spend with herself would help her to think…to clear her head, but all that went through her mind was the enjoyable afternoon she spent with Melvin. Not that anything special had sparked between them; it was just nice to spend time sitting and talking with someone of the opposite sex. What made her evening worse is that she didn't enjoy herself. Everywhere she went, she kept peeping over her shoulder and through the masses of sea fairing cruisers to see if any of the male figures resembled Melvin. *'Funny'*, she thought. *It's been years since I've seen or even thought of that man, and in just one day his presence, his nearness has become so familiar to me.*

Betty felt a little annoyed with herself. She would probably be asleep when her two roommates got in, and since they were leaving out for their shore excursion in the morning, she thought she would search out Melvin–that is if he was still on board. She wanted to apologies for not showing up for dinner. It wasn't that they had a date or anything like that, or even that she owed him an apology, but she was beginning to feel that they, well…that they made a connection with each other. She couldn't help but wonder if he was feeling the same thing.

After dinner Melvin went to sit in the Piano Lounge. He had muddled through his meal, but really couldn't remember what he had eaten. Anita and Vicky said they were going to the Calypso Lounge to rejoin some gentlemen they had met earlier, and invited him to come along. "Who knows", Anita said, "you might get lucky and meet a lady you can *get* with." He knew from the way she said get with, that she had no idea what kind of man he was, or the kind of woman he was interested in. Besides, he had already met a lady he liked.

Melvin sat at the *'Boogie'* style table and listened while the pianist tickled out a soft jazzy tune. He wasn't a drinking man, but he ordered a Tom Collin's anyway. He tried to convince himself that he needed something stronger than a coke to help him think. But, what he actually wanted was to see Betty again. It wasn't just because things didn't go as planned with Beverly, or out of 'throw-back' memories of their high school days; he *really* enjoyed her company. If she had come to dinner tonight he was going to see if she wanted to stroll around the deck a time or two, or maybe watch the 'on-board' outdoor movie with him, but she didn't come, so he didn't go.

On his way back to his cabin Melvin thought about tomorrow being Christmas Eve. His previous plans concerning Bev were no longer in the picture. It occurred to him how silly it was for him to make all those plans involving someone who never gave him any reason to think that she thought of him in a romantic way.

When he reached his room, the ship's newsletter was laying on his freshly made bed. His eyes fell on the bold print reminding cruisers who planned to attend the Captain's Gala Christmas Eve Extravaganza to reserve their spot by purchasing their tickets. Not that he had a date or anything now that Beverly seemed to take interest in the man she'd met on board. However, he checked the article again to see when the cut off time was. It said tickets were going quickly, and the last chance to purchase the few remaining ones would be tomorrow morning by 9:00am.

A surge of optimism flowed through his veins. He had to get up to the purser's desk first thing in the morning to purchase two tickets. He would ask Betty if she wanted to go with him. There he was going out on the limb again—taking things for granted. *Maybe she had her own plans. Maybe she had secretly met with someone else tonight. After all, Anita and Vicky could have been wrong.*

Melvin showered and went to bed.  He had often prayed (maybe not often enough) that God would grant him another chance at happiness; that he'd meet a *good* wife. Up until now he thought *that* woman was Beverly. She was the one he admired and wished he could be the man in her life, even when she was still married to his good friend. Melvin realized that that was *coveting*. Now, it got him to wondering if it was truly Beverly that he was admiring, or was it something she stood for? Melvin woke from his sleep in the middle of the night and was confused when he realized he had dreamed again about having a wife, but he could have sworn the woman in the dream this time was Betty… not Beverly.

———⁓———

Beverly lay across her bed in the early morning hours still praying for sleep, but too many thoughts were running through her head.  Her *uncertain heart* was filled with the expectation that this man might actually care for her, but she was afraid to open up to that happening. She had to smile at the irony, or craziness of it all. Three days ago she was sitting at home not even thinking about this vacation being a romantic interlude, and now here she was on a cruise ship where two men had shown a strong interest in her. And, the only thing running through her mind was how to avoid confronting either one of them. *'Hello, what's wrong with you girl'? A voice came penetrating through her mind. 'It's Christmas'! You struck out on this venture for three main reasons: To try something different, to get away from home, and to put a little joy back in your life. Well* (the voice was almost audible), *Get out there and do it!*

At that moment Beverly was more peeved with herself than ever because it dawned on her that she had not kept her promises to God—to trust Him with all her needs and desires. The very scripture she had quoted over and over again when she first decided she would break out of her mold and her everyday routine was, "God has not given me a spirit of fear, but a spirit of power, of love, and of a sound mind."2 Timothy 1:7. *"Yeah"*, she thought as her heavy eyelids began to give way to sleep, *'that didn't last long'. Whatever this is, I know it's not anything I've planned, because I didn't have a plan. Well Lord, I guess I'll go with the flow, and run on to see what the end shall be.* Beverly smiled to herself because she tied the old religious saying in to fit her present situation.

A few hours later, Beverly woke in a jolt! She knew she had been dreaming because of the impossible craziness that seemed to be happening to her. Some portions of her dream were blissfully romantic. However, at one part in the dream she was walking down the middle aisle of a church (she assumed it was a wedding–*her wedding*). She was wearing the colorful ruffled skirt and the 'tee' shirt she wore to the *'Sail-a-way'* deck party. She still had on her sandals and sunglasses, and the only added feature was a bridal veil.

She was slowly moving up the aisle, and the bald Caucasian guy wearing swim trunks jumped out from the crowded pew and started *Tangoing* toward her. Then, the Hispanic man jumped in front of him, and was exotically moving his body in very suggestive motions. She began looking from side to side for a way of escape, and out of the blue, there was Brandon standing at the altar with his arms extended out towards her.

She began to run up to the altar, and just when she was within arm's reach of him, Emily stepped out from the pew on the front row. She stood next to a large lever. She gave her mother a big smirk, pulled the lever back, and Beverly fell through a trap door in the floor.

Beverly guessed it was the sudden feeling of falling into nothingness that caused her to wake so suddenly. She shook her head back and forth in an effort to clear her mind. "What in the world was that all about?" *Dreams are strange things,* she thought. They are such a collaboration of mixed up feelings and fantasy's; and then again, they also have a way of unfolding a bit of truth.

———⌇———

Clearly, of the two ladies, Anita was taking the evening by storm. She was loud, boisterous, and unrestrained. After dinner the girls met back up with Kevin and Terrance, who *evidently* was as much of a side kick to Kevin as she was to Anita. Vicky didn't mind having a good time, but Anita was ridiculous. She was down-right embarrassing. Vicky knew she was paired off with Terrance because Anita made it perfectly clear that she wanted to be with Kevin. Vicky had a strong suspicion that Kevin could have been a married man, but her friend didn't care. He was tall, slim (but buff), had brown wavy hair, a caramel colored complexion, and hazel eyes that drew you to him from across the room.

Oh, Terrance wasn't a bad looking guy either. He was about 5ft. 10 inches tall, and had a very athletic physique. He wore his hair cut short and trimmed, and he had very attractive dark brown eyes; although there seemed to be a note of sadness behind them. Vicky noticed he didn't wear a wedding band, but neither did Kevin. The difference between the two of them was, that she could tell that Terrance hadn't wore one for a long time, if he had worn one at all.

Vicky guessed that by being a plain Jane, you get a lot of opportunities to just sit and observe people, and it appeared that Terrance was not having a good time. She only hoped it wasn't because he got stuck with her–the ugly *one*. At any rate, she could tell his personality was not the wild flamboyant type like his friend. They sat and had a couple of drinks (of which two was her limit) and talked about how they met each of the friends they happened to be cruising with. This was his third cruise, and Vicky's second. Their attention turned to Kevin and Anita, and Terrance and Vicky humorously commented that they both needed to stay sober because they were sure they would be the *lean-on,* their friends would need in order to get back to their cabins tonight.

# Chapter 15

As soon as Brandon woke, he sensed something different about the ship. That was it! The soft hum of the churning engines had ceased. This ship must have made port some time during the early morning hours. He heard the sound of running water coming from the bathroom, and surmised that it was Tommy taking his early morning shower.

Brandon felt for his wristwatch on the nightstand between the two beds, and tried to focus his eyes on the dial. It was a few minutes after seven o'clock. Tommy emerged through the small narrow doors of the bathroom with a towel wrapped around his midsection. Brandon noticed his son's muscular chest and his tight rib cage, and in a kind of a fatherly covet, he remembered when he looked like that years ago. It wasn't that he had let himself go; it's just that some things come along with the aging process.

"Hey Pops, you going to lay there all day?" Tommy didn't give his dad chance to answer before he started talking again. "I'm going up on the deck to see what the Island looks like. You want to grab some breakfast with me?" "Well, not if you're ready to go this minute." Tommy came back out of the bathroom wearing his jockey shorts and a "Tee" shirt; the old-fashioned kind that in today's lingo is called a 'wife-beater'... He headed to the closet and pulled out a pair of white linen pants, and a colorful floral shirt.

Brandon looked at his son and thought he'd tease him a little. "Your mighty spruced up and smelling good just to go to breakfast with your old dad." Tommy started right in trying to think up an excuse for the well-made plans he had for himself and a certain young lady he met. "Well… You see Pops, I thought you were getting in pretty tight with the lady I saw you with last night so…" In the middle of his sentence he turned to see the smile on his dad's face. "Aw, see Pops, you wrong for that." Tommy moved toward his dad who by now was sitting on the edge of his bed.

He grabbed the towel he had slung over the back of the desk chair, and through it at his father. Brandon ducked, but was laughing so hard he almost couldn't speak. "Man, who do you think you're fooling? Don't you know that I know you by now? I've only been your father for thirty two-year. You may have a few moves of your own, but basically everything else, I've taught you." "What! You taught me?" The father and son engaged in a little friendly banter. Brandon told Tommy to go ahead with his day and not to worry about him, because he had plans of his own. Tommy stopped and got serious for a moment. "I know pop. I've been checking her out, and let me say, she seems pretty nice."

~

Betty was glad that Anita and Vicki were going ashore. Her original plan was to have a spa day, but now she wanted to peruse the ship in search of Melvin. Her friends were anxious to leave, but Betty insisted on saying a prayer over them first. After they left, she dressed in a hurry in order to catch the breakfast buffet, and then she would venture on to look for Melvin. She hoped he was still aboard the ship. Betty helped herself to a hearty breakfast that included some fruit. Now she felt a little silly not knowing what she would say to Melvin even if she did run into him.

From where she sat she could see the beautiful island. She took out her cell phone to check for the time. It was about 9:30 AM in the morning. The sky was blue, the sun was shining and from where she sat, she could see the activity going on near the port. She took a few pictures and stuffed the phone back into her shirt pocket. A gentleman's voice coming from behind gave her a start. "Ah ha! I see you found our favorite table". *Betty was dumbfounded.*

"May I?" Melvin said, nodding his head toward the empty chair across from her. Betty gave a pleasing smile. She was swallowing hard trying to work past the lump in her throat. Melvin removed his various dishes from the tray, and put the tray on the vacant table next to them. He slid into the seat facing her and said, "Good Morning." He excused himself and Betty watched as he said a silent prayer over his food. While she waited, the thing that was going through her mind was the statement he said about *our favorite* table. *Was this the same table that they sat at the other day? She couldn't remember.* When he raised his head, she joined him in a 'verbal' amen. Melvin asked if she always joined in on the Amen after other people said the grace, and she said; "Only when I forgot to say my own, then I have to ditto in on someone else's." They both laughed, and begin to have a delightful conversation.

Melvin told her he really missed her at dinner Wednesday night. Betty felt bad about it too, but what excuse could she give—that she was chicken, and didn't want Anita and Vicky to notice that she and Melvin had already become acquainted with each other. While they were having breakfast, Melvin had two things on his mind. One, spending more time with Betty today, and the other thing was to find the right time to ask her to the Christmas Eve ball. He had already purchased the tickets this morning, and hoped she'd go. Melvin brought up the subject again of last night's dinner.

He wasn't trying to pry any information about her date, or whereabouts. He was just trying to get a lead into asking her if she had plans for today, better yet, for this evening. He said, "I saw you taking some pictures with your phone. Would you mind if I took a picture with you?" He pulled his camera phone out of his pant pocket. "Now, let's see", he said. We need someone to take the picture for us. If I may borrow your phone, we'll both have pictures of this memorable face; not unless you want me to send you one from my phone. That way we'll both have pictures of us cursing" Betty handed him her phone.

She wasn't ready to exchange contact information just yet. Melvin stopped one of the Servers and asked her to take their pictures. He didn't want *'selfies'* because he wanted to get the both of them sitting at the table together. He thanked the young lady and returned Betty's phone to her. "This is much better", he said. The ship's photographer took several shots of everyone at their tables last night. I know I was in a few of them, but I didn't have a desire to take home photos of the company I was with." Betty knew he was speaking about her friends.

Melvin took advantage of the opening he had provided "You know, if you want to take some beautiful pictures we can go ashore together, and look around. As a matter of fact, I read in the newsletter about the Water Island Ferry. We both can get some great pictures, and it's only $10 per person for round-trip." *After he said it, he wondered if it made him sound like he was a cheapskate not wanting to pay for her ride too.* Evidently, it didn't sound that way to Betty. She thought it was a great idea. Since her plans had change for the day, Betty wanted to change her outfit and put on some comfortable shoes for the excursion, and so did Melvin. They agreed to meet back down at the tour exit ramp in an hour.

---

A second sense nudge at Vicki that caused her to feel uneasy about the day. Coming down the ramp from the ship, they spotted Kevin and Terrance waiting for them. Kevin was waving his hands in the air, and calling their names to get their attention. Vicki and Anita stopped a few seconds to pause for the ships photographer, then they continued on down the ramp.

Vicki directed her attention toward Terrance. She wasn't sure if what she saw was a smile on his face, or was he squinting because of the sun? She was pleasantly surprised when what seemed like a squint at first, turned into a smile. Vicki always paid close attention to the way she dressed, drawing ones eye toward her good features. She learned to be creative with her hair and makeup. There was nothing she could do about the facial features she acquired from her parents. She had given thought to the idea of cosmetic surgery; especially the one that could slender the skin around the corner of the eyes. But, she not only heard, but also looked up online some of the case studies on those procedures and found that the results were far from perfect. She decided she'd rather be 'popped-eyed' than to be mangled or blind.

As for her teeth, she wished she had done something about them year before. She could have worn braces which probably would have added to the unbecoming features of her face, but that wasn't a very appealing idea. She also could have had four of her front teeth pulled, and had a bridge made. Neither one of the ideas suited her at that time, so she ended up doing nothing at all. Now that she had met someone she thought could be interested in her, she wished she had taken care of those little details.

# Chapter 16

Brandon had the morning to himself, and it was already dragging on, but his aim was to find Beverly as soon as he could. It was going to be a pretty warm day, and he would have donned a tee-shirt and Bermuda shorts if he were at home. But today he chose to wear a pair of white cotton pants, a solid color 'tee' under an unbuttoned white short-sleeve linen shirt. He had always been a little self-conscious of his slightly bowed legs. He smiled to himself thinking about the way Grace used to think that a bow-legged man had sex appeal. She use to *say* women liked tall men who had slightly bowed legs, and walked with a swagger. Brandon never considered, or even admitted that he walked with a slight swagger, but his wife used to teased him saying, "You always said that Tommy was a chip off the old block, and that includes the walk that he has… just like his daddy!"

Brandon checked his wallet to be sure he had his I.D., his Ship -n-Sail boarding card, a few traveler's checks, and some US currency in small bills. He couldn't believe how nervous he was. He hadn't felt this way since he first met Grace. *This is crazy,* he thought. *I've got butterflies in my stomach!* He wanted their day to be light and easy. So for that reason, there wouldn't be much walking the Island. It was already hot. He would pay the driver to take them to see a few interesting sights. They would take some pictures, and then ask the 'cabby' to find a nice *cool* place so they could have some iced tea, or lemonade. Of course, if she wanted to shop in a store or two, he wouldn't object.

He asked Beverly, and she said the outing was fine. She told him she had done all the shopping she was going to do for her family before she left home—although she thought she might pick up some souvenirs in the gift shop. Brandon had something in mind that he wanted to give Beverly as a Christmas gift, but he wasn't going to purchase it at any of the shops that were on the Island. He knew the cost of almost everything would be doubled. What he wanted to get her was expensive enough as it was, no use throwing money away. Besides that, he didn't want to purchase it while she was with him. He wanted this gift to be a surprise.

All in all, the day went well. They got back to the ship around 4pm. He gave the cab driver a generous tip, and helped Beverly out of the taxi. He knew he would be taking a chance, but after he closed the door he continued to hold her hand. She didn't seem to mind. She even gave him a sweet smile. Brandon's heart and pulse rate began to elevate. He tried to remain calm, cool, and collected. *"Don't blow it now"*, he said to himself. They held hands from the taxicab all the way to the entrance ramp of the ship. Brandon finalized their plans for the evening; if she wanted the few minutes to herself after dinner, he would pick her up at her cabin around 8:00pm.

They arrive at the elevator and waited for its descent. When the doors open, Brandon turned to faced Beverly. He was being drawn to this beautiful woman, but he resisted the urge to do what he felt like doing. Instead, he did something very *gallant*. He raised the hand he was still holding to his lips–gave the back of her hand a gentle kiss and a loving squeeze, and then released it. "I'll see you tonight", he said. Beverly got in the elevator, and the glass doors closed in front of her.

It was when she got the top level that Beverly realized she had pushed the` *up*' button instead of going one level down to her floor. She could only hope that Brandon had gone to run the errand he told her about, and was not still standing on the Promenade deck. However, just by happenstance, Melvin was coming down the grand staircase and stopped when he saw the two of them together. He observed the scene, and despite how the thought he should have felt about what occurred, there was still a tinge of jealousy running through his veins. None the less, he had to make himself feel good about the way things were turning out for Beverly.

Vicki wanted to find the first vacant ladies room she could find, and then seek out a place of solitude but she had to help Terrance back to the cabin with Anita. Terrance said she could wait if she thought her friend was in any danger with him, but she knew Anita was safe back on the ship and all Vicky wanted to do was to be alone. Vicky was not just embarrassed, but totally distraught with her friend. She went to the library and sat in one of those cushion horseshoe-shaped leather chairs. The day so far had been a complete disaster, but it could have been worse if Terrance had not interceded. She was grateful Betty had prayed over them before they left. It was *true* that he and Kevin had taken this cruise before, but Kevin was with his wife.

It seems their marriage was headed toward divorce, and he convinced her to go on a cruise. Terrance said that at that time he had secretly brought another lady-friend along on the same cruise. Kevin deserted his wife, leaving her on board while he went ashore with the other woman. He and the other woman had been having an affair. When he tried to break it off she blackmailed him into paying for a ticket for her to come on the cruise, or else she was going to *spill their whole sorted affair to his wife!*

While on the cruise Kevin received some inside information from one of the men aboard ship about a motel he could visit to have a *'good time'* no questions asked. Terrance and his lady friend toured the Island, and not knowing what Kevin had in mind returned to the ship. It just so happened that Kevin and the other woman never boarded on time, and had to board the ship at the next port. His wife was furious! That wasn't all that happened.

During the motel visit, the girlfriend was slipped some drugs, and several men were allowed to visit the room to participate in a *good* time with her. When the two of them finally boarded the ship, she stayed shut up in her cabin for the rest of the cruise. Terrance said he believed  Kevin threatened her; saying that if she tried to expose him, he would tell everyone in the office that when they got on the Island she ducked out on him, and went with some guys she'd met in a bar. He said he would say that she went willingly with them, and he spent so long searching for her that he had to call the ship. He did call the ship, but it was to say he lost his wallet and ID on the Island, and by the time he backtracked his steps to the restaurant where he left it, it was past time for boarding.

He also told the girl that he would tell everyone that she told him a lie about taking the cruise to visit her mother, but didn't have enough money to finish paying for the ticket; so he helped her out. Terrance told Vicky that everyone else might have believed him, but his wife didn't. *"Somehow,* he said, *wives know"!*

Vicky wasn't sure how long she had been sitting in the library. It must've been awhile, because hunger pains were emerging. On the Island Kevin and Anita left the two of them hours before noon. She guessed it was at that time that things begin to happen. Vicky knew that Terrance seemed jittery and inattentive to her, but that was something she was used to.

When a young boy and a girl came in the library, Vicky got up and moved to another quiet spot. She wasn't quite ready to go back to the cabin yet. She was almost sure Anita was still passed out, or if she was awake, she was probably angry and embarrassed. She just wasn't ready to face her. *'She should be grateful that Terrance came along when he did',* she thought. Thank God he had a conscience, even if his friend didn't.

Vicky thought back recalling the incident afresh and anew. She and Terrance had just begun their lunch when he jumped up from the table and said, "Come on. We've got to go"! He slapped some money down on the table and started to move. He almost snatched her up with the chair still under her, and ran outside to hail a taxi. She had no idea what was going on, but knew she wasn't in any danger with him. He gave the driver the name of a motel that wasn't far from where they had lunch. They arrived there in less than five minutes. He told her to stay in the taxi, and told the driver to wait for him, and to keep the motor running.

A few minutes later he emerged from the motel lobby with Anita. She looked a mess. Terrance had one arm around her waist, and her other arm he had circled around his neck. He was holding her up, bracing her body against his as she struggled to stand. It looked like she had no cognizance of how to put one foot in front of the other. Vicky remembered jumping from the taxi to help just as Kevin came ripping out behind them. Terrance told her to get Anita into the Cab, and to lock the door. *What in the world was going on?* The two men were definitely having a serious confrontation, and she was hoping it wouldn't come to blows.

Anita began reaching for the door handle, and tried to get out of the taxi cab. Vicky had to pull her back with force. Anita said something to the effect of "Hey, get your stinking hands off me" through her slurred speech. Anita could really mean at times, but at least she didn't cuss her out. By that time Terrance was on his way back to the Cab. He quickly opened the passenger front door, and almost before he got seated, he told the driver to move out. The 'cabby' peeled rubber, and left!

They headed for the pier where their ship was docked. When we arrived Terrance asked Vicky if it would be alright for him to help get Anita back to their cabin, that it would look better if a man was assisting a woman who appeared to be drunk; rather than two ladies struggling together. He said he was going to explain a few things to Anita once they got back to the room, and hoped that through her fuzzy head she was able to understand some of what he had to say. He told Vicky that Anita would probably be *'out of it'* for a few hours—most likely in dead sleep. Still, he said, if Vicky didn't want to stay in the cabin, it would be a good idea if she came back to check on her friend in a little while.

# Chapter 17

Melvin didn't want to waste much time. He wanted to find something nice for Betty and, since he had asked her to the Christmas Eve Ball, he wanted to surprise her with an unexpected Christmas present. But, what should he get? It had been so long since he brought a woman a personal gift, he wasn't sure what to buy. By the time he and his ex-wife got their divorce, he had stopped trying to please her with '*niceties*' because no matter what he did, she didn't appreciate anything.

---

Brandon found himself in one of the ship's nicest Couture shops. Looking around brought back memories of how lovely, and feminine the fairer sex is. He remembered the way Gracie would '*oooh', and ahh*' with delight whenever he surprised her with a little '*just because I love you gift*'. Brandon stopped to call his thoughts back into reality. He could almost bet he was standing there with a silly smile on his face.

The shop had almost everything a woman would desire, but he knew what he was looking for—*White Linen* perfume. That was the perfume Beverly was wearing the night of the play. He recognized the allure of its sensual aroma as it drew fond romantic thoughts of *his* dear Gracie. He had brought it for her many a time. It was her favorite. It was ironic that Beverly wore the same perfume. Now that he thought about it; why would he buy her something she obviously already had? He searched the boutique to see what else he could get for her, but couldn't get the perfume out of his mind. *He hoped it was not because of his remembrance of Gracie.*

It seemed as if he wasn't the only male on board doing some last minute Christmas shopping. The small boutique was crowded. Some of the men paddled around with confused looks on their faces; while others gave unspoken, knowingly glances to one another that said…*getting this extra last minute gift is going to make Christmas morning a whole lot cheerier for me!* It was virtually impossible not to bump into a fellow shopper, and that's exactly what happened at one of the jewelry counters.

Brandon bent down to get a closer look at the locket inside the case, and bumped the guy behind him. Both men turned to apologize to each other, and there stood Brandon and Melvin face to face. A few awkward seconds passed between them before Melvin spoke up first. "Well, fancy meeting you here. Although I'm not surprised seeing how well you and Beverly seem to be getting along." Brandon couldn't resist replying in a pretentious, challenging tone of voice. "I hope that doesn't ruin any of your previous plans."

Melvin picked up on the insinuating remark. "Look *Bro*, I deserved that, but I've apologized to Beverly and asked for her forgiveness. She's accepted, and all is forgiven. We are on a cruise ship, so we're bound to run into each other once in a while. What do you want me to do…jump ship in the middle of the ocean?" Brandon gave a plastered smile, but refused to answer. Melvin gave Brandon a brotherly pat on the shoulder. "You know, he said, the good Lord may have had another reason for getting me on this cruise, because it sure wasn't for what I originally thought it was." He was still wrestling with the personal agenda he had planned for himself. Melvin shook off the reminder. He removed his hand from Brandon's shoulder and stuffed it in his pocket.

"Well", he said, "We're both here and we're both trying to buy something for two different ladies." Brandon's ears perked up

when he heard the words *two different ladies.*
His conscious was relieved, but he tried not to
show it on his face. "Soo, he slowly said, you're
not here looking to buy something for Beverly."
"Ironically no. I'm trying to buy something for
a lady I met on board. She's a lady I went to
high school with years ago. We ran into each
other at dinner, and the more we talked the
more I realized how comfortable I was talking
with her. We went ashore to view the Island,
and she agreed to go to the Christmas Ball with
me tonight. So here I am trying to find
something appropriate for a beginning
friendship, but nothing that would suggest she
*owes* me something for the gift, or the evening
if you know what I mean."

Brandon understood exactly what he
meant, and was willing to help out. He extended
his hand toward Melvin. "Friends", his said.
Melvin returned the gesture, "friends." The men
released their hand-shake, and Brandon said,
"Let me show you something I was just looking
at over here, I was thinking of getting one for
Beverly, and maybe this will work for your lady
too."

---

Vicky picked up the telephone in the
library and dialed her cabin. Thank God it was

Betty who answered. Betty told her that Anita
was still a bit groggy, but she ordered some hot
coffee and a light snack from the room service
menu. Betty sounded some-what worried. But
before Vicky got off the phone she shared a
little of what happened on the Island. She told
her friend to go ahead and start to prepare for
her evening out, and she would be back to the
cabin in just a little bit. Vicky didn't go so far
as to mention any names because it wouldn't
have meant much to Betty anyway. She placed
the phone back on its cradle, and sat at a table
near one of the round porthole windows that
looked out over the now rippling waters. The
movement of the ship, and the distant sound of
Christmas music ebbed a calm settling in her
uneasy spirit.

"Man, you're a pretty hard person to
catch up with when you don't want to be
found!" The familiar voice startled her and
caught her off guard. She turned to see Terrance
towering over her. Vicky was stricken. She
tried to move her lips, but no voice seemed to
follow. "I'm sorry, Terrance said, I didn't mean
to startle you." Vicky just stared blankly. "Are
you okay?" Again, Vicky tried to respond, but
her larynx clamed shut. All she could do was to
nod her head *'yes'*. *Why is this man talking to
me? The games they tried to play ended hours
ago. The charade is over. He doesn't have to*

*act interested in me anymore.* Terrance slid in the chair across from her. He gave her a warming smile and asked if she had checked in on her friend.

Vicky began to speak, but her voice sounded distant and muffled in her ears—like what happens to you when your ears plug up on an airplane. "I didn't go to the room, but I just called, and our other roommate was there. She was tending to Anita with some black coffee and something lite to eat from Room Service."

"Speaking of room service, Terrance said, I don't know about you. But I'm mighty hungry. I rushed you off in the middle of a spectacular lunch." Vicky gave an agreeing smile; afraid to say anything else. "Well, I tell you what. How 'bout you and me having dinner tonight? He looked down at his watch, let's say around 7:00 O'clock. That'll give us time to freshen up and change." It was then that she noticed he was still wearing the clothes he had on when they left the ship this morning. Terrance followed Vicky's eyes as they rested upon his rumpled garments.

"Yeah, I've been trying to find you for most of the afternoon. I wanted to see if you were all right." "Thank you. I'm feeling much better", she said."

He rose from his seat and said, "We probably have different dinning seating's, so why don't I call for you at your cabin, and we can eat at 'Breezes of the Sea'; that is if you don't mind." Vicky told Terrance he really didn't have to ask her to dinner to make up for anything that happened this afternoon. He put his hand on the back of her chair; indicating his gentlemanly manners in helping a lady out of her seat.

Vicky braced one leg back against the rim of the chair and gave it a slight push as she stood. Terrance's eyes met her face, and looking in her eyes he said. "I didn't ask you to dinner because I had to. I asked you to dinner because I *wanted* to." He turned and walked across the room, and Vicky stood there in shock. She was too stunned to move.

Terrance scurried off to find an open gift shop. *This is Christmas Eve* he said to himself, *and I have a dinner date with a very nice lady.* He wanted to purchase two gifts; one for Vicky tonight, and one for her to open on Christmas Day.

# Chapter 18

Betty's heart went out to Anita. She listened while Anita retold what she could remember of her horrific experience. She even said she didn't realize, or suspect that she was in any danger right up to the last minute. Betty asked her friend if she wanted prayer, and Anita said yes. Betty knew her friend needed the Lord in her life, and heaven knows she needed salvation—however at this time, she only felt lead to pray for the healing of the many hurts in her life. Betty knew that Anita put up a good front, but there were some deeply seeded issues in her life that had not been resolved, and no amount of alcohol, or fast living could help her run away from it.

Her prayer was filled with compassion and empathy. She didn't judge or condemn. Anita's heart began to melt, and she didn't interrupt with her usual quips and defenses. Her tears flowed freely, and she apologized for the way she often treated her and Vicky, *especially Vicky.* She said she never had to practice being nice to people, because people were always nice to her first because of her looks. She was always pretty. Anita raised her head to look at

Betty and said, "Although it takes a little more makeup now-a- days." They both had a good laugh behind that.

Betty let Anita in on her secret meetings with Melvin, and told her he invited her to the Christmas Eve Ball tonight. She said she wanted to look nice, but she didn't bring anything that fancy to wear. That was right up Anita's alley. Something special to wear wasn't nothing but a *word.*

Vicky entered the cabin to find her roommates had clothes strewn out all over the beds. They were searching through Anita's wardrobe trying to find something appropriate for Betty to wear to the Ball. Before Vicky could ask what was going on, Anita ran to her friend, threw both arms around her shoulders and apologized to her profusely. Betty grabbed the tissue box from the end table, and stood close by. Their tears flowed. Afterwards, Vicky went to the closet and pulled out a few of her own garments, and threw them in the mix. "Well, I might as well get in on this wardrobe makeover. I'm not going to the Ball, but I do have a Christmas Eve dinner date with a man named Terrance."

Anita and Betty stopped in their tracks. All of a sudden a mirage of high pitched squeals erupted from the both of them. They hugged each other in a threesome circle jumping around the room. *This time no snide remarks about Vicky's looks came out of Anita's mouth.*

When the excitement died down they started mixing and matching their wardrobes together to come up with the perfect outfit for each of the ladies to wear. Anita got them all to laughing by saying, "If this isn't a *true* fairytale, I don't know what is. I feel like 'Cinderella' helping my two step *'Sistas'* get dressed for the Ball; so if any of you find a real prince out there, you better hang on to him for as long as you can! Lord knows I've messed up my chances with mine."

———— ∾ ————

Tommy shook his head back and forth in disbelief. "Man Pops, you're pitiful! I can't believe you're this nervous over a date with a woman. But, what I really can't believe is that you rented a Tuxedo from the men's shop. I'm flabbergasted that you spent *that* kind of money." Brandon looked at his son. "Well, what did you expect me to do, go to a formal Ball in my Bermuda shorts? I didn't come prepared for *anything* like this." Tommy laughed again. "So, by *any of this* are you talking about meeting a lady, or spending a romantic evening at a Christmas dance?"

Brandon gave Tommy sort of a questioning smirk. "Neither one, I guess. It all feels kind of odd; weird…you know what I Mean?" Tommy got out of the chair to assist his dad with his formal bow tie. His voice dropped to a more serious tone. "Look dad, I know you've been going through a rough time since Mom passed away. She was your love, your life. It's only been three and a half years, (Tommy paused) but I think this lady's okay. I mean…what I'm trying to say is that it's alright if you find interest in another woman. I can tell you have some feelings for her, and you've got to admit, it was fate the way you'll met. Pops, I know this is going to sound funny, but you need to release yourself from feeling guilty about caring for another woman…it's okay."

The two men stood face to face for a few seconds, and Brandon saw before him a grown up man. Not knowing what to do at such a tender moment, Brandon took the lighter side of the coin and said, "Thanks Dad. Now can I borrow the keys to go to the dance?" The words may have come out in a playful sarcastic way, but the genuine hugs between father and son took them to a higher level in their relationship with each other.

———————————⁓———————————

Beverly sprayed some perfume at the nap of her neck, behind her earlobes, and across her shoulders. She waited a few seconds and then pulled the spaghetti straps to her semi-formal dress up around her exposed shoulders. She stepped back to view herself in the floor length mirror on the bathroom door. She was satisfied with her appearance, but not so much with her emotions.

*Okay, 'Miss' Lady. You broke away from your traditional routine because you said you wanted to experience something different..., but not this different,* she thought. *Look at you. You're going on a date with a man you just met a few days ago—and on a cruise of all things! Suppose you never see him again?* Beverly thought out loud, "So, suppose I don't ever see him again. What difference will that make?"

The problem was, she was pretty sure she would like to see him again. *Heck,* she thought, *I don't even know where the man lives.* She turned back to the dresser and spritzed her hair with some of the perfume, and her eye caught the level of perfume that was left in the bottle. The contents was very low, but that was all she brought with her. She had already spent so much on Christmas shopping and preparing for the cruise, she didn't want to spend money on purchasing a new bottle. That could always wait until she got home; besides it might even be on sale by then.


The Christmas plant on the round table in the corner served as her little Christmas tree. It was holding up nicely, and to make it a little more festive she purchased two pare of shepherd-hook earrings from the gift shop. They were replicas of little Christmas bulbs; green and red. She hung them on the tree to give the room more of a holiday feeling. It helped some, but it was Beverly that needed the boast. She missed being with family.

# Chapter 19

Beverly grabbed the small box and the envelope off the table and put them in her evening bag. She made sure she had her room card-key, her lipstick, and her compact. Now that her perfume had settled, she went to the vanity and put on her jewelry. Her eyes spotted the tiny box of breath freshener strips lying next to some hair pins, so she picked it up and threw it in her purse too. She took a quick look at her watch, and knew that Brandon would be there in five-or-so minutes to escort her to the Ball. That would give her enough time to say a little prayer for confidence, and to use the rest room one last time.

Before she could move, the phone sounded two short rings. She answered it, and Brandon's voice came through the receiver. "Good evening Beverly Sparks, do you need a little more time, or can I be at your door in about five minutes?" Bev drew in a long nervous breath and said, "Your timing is perfect, I'll be ready."

——— ∾ ———

Terrance answered the knock on the cabin door. It certainly wasn't anyone he expected. Terrance tried not to spend much time in the room since the aggressive riff between he and Kevin this afternoon. He only came back a short while ago in order to shower, shave, and dress for his dinner date with Vicky. Kevin was still fuming, so they shared as few words as possible.

The two gentlemen at the door were very official looking. One of them looked to be the ship's Chief Officer, and the other a security person of some sort because of his badge. Terrance was not only concerned, but confused. The expression must have been evident on his face. The ship's Chief Officer spoke up first. "Good evening Mr. Weber sir. Sorry to disturbed your evening. We're here to see Kevin Stephens. I believe he's your cabin mate." Kevin moved from the bed, and came to the middle of the floor. "Hey, what's going on here? What do you want to see me about?" The security officer stepped inside the room. He was about six foot four inches tall, of a muscular build; and was carrying a sidearm. Terrance thought that to be quite unusual.

"Sir, we would like for you to come with us, we have a few questions we would like to ask you." Kevin's demeanor changed instantly. "Hey, I'm not going nowhere with you guys until you tell me what this is all about!" "Sir, the officer said, we would rather not divulge any personal information here in front of Mr. Weber."

Kevin shot a glance at Terrance. Terrance knew exactly what it was about, but he didn't say anything. The look on Kevin's face turned to one of rage. In an instant he lunged toward Terrance, and before he could strike out at him the officer bolted between them to defuse the attack. "Why you dirty dog", he shouted. Terrance stepped back. "Man, what are you talking about?" "You know-good 'n well what I'm talking about." "Yes I do, and you got it all wrong. I'm not the one who ratted on you!"

The Chief Officer moved into the circle. "He's right Mr. Stevens. Our report came from the motel manager who viewed his security cameras after you and Mr. Weber left the premises with the victim. They recognized two of the men who entered the motel lobby as local petty drug dealers—amongst other things. Then the camera showed them going into the room you reserved." The Security Officer chimed in saying, "It also caught Mr. Weber here entering the room about ten minutes later. Of course we couldn't see what went on inside the room, however immediately after your friend here entered, the other two men came running out, half clothed. Less than a minute later, we viewed Mr. Weber manually dragging the victim out of the room. By the way, it was the two men who ratted on you, and they informed the St. Thomas police that this wasn't your first time in dealing with them in this manner."

Kevin was speechless. The Officers said that if he cooperated with them peacefully, they would not cuff him as they walked through the ship to his new quarters. They informed him that he would be held under guard in a secure place where he couldn't interact with the other passengers. When the ship docked at San Juan in the morning, he would be handed over to the proper officials.

Since Anita refused to press assault charges against him, the cruise line could only hold him on charges of *'Endangerment'* with intent to harm a fellow passenger. They also said he would be banned from ever booking passage on any of their cruise ships anywhere inside, or outside of the United States. When the officers left the cabin with Kevin, they asked Terrance to pack all of Kevin's things, and to sit his suitcase outside the door; someone would be by to pick it up. Terrance's guess was that they didn't want him to know where Kevin was going to being held.

———————⁓———————

Anita was glad that her roommates would be out for the evening. Melvin had already come by to escort Betty to the Ball, and Terrance phoned the room to say he had been detained, but he should be there in about twenty minutes. Vicky looked worried when she hung the phone up, but Anita reassured her that a man wouldn't call to say he would be a little late if he didn't plan to come at all. In that case he probably just wouldn't have called at all. She reassured her friend by saying that Terrance–unlike his friend, seemed to be a man of his word and she had nothing to worry about.

Sure enough, he knocked on the door around 8:15pm. Vicky wore one of her own dresses, some elegant holiday pumps, and a sequined wrap she borrowed from Anita. Anita helped the girls with new hair-dos, and added a little extra sparkle to their make-up. It was definitely worth the extra effort, because when each of their dates showed up at the cabin, the men's approval showed in their eyes, and was voiced by complimentary words. Terrance asked Anita if she was going to be alright. He didn't mention anything that had occurred between her and Kevin, but she knew what he meant. He also didn't mention what just went down with Kevin and the ship's security. He just felt it wasn't the right time.

Anita was hungry, but wasn't sure if to venture out of the cabin, or not. She didn't want to order from the limited menu offered by room service, yet she didn't want to take the chance of running into Kevin. Betty was in the room earlier when the two Officers came by, so they asked to speak with her alone. They walked to the open lounge area just outside of the corridor. It was amazing to her the way they ID'd her from the motel surveillance cameras, and tracked her down by her ship-n-sail pass. The ships cameras showed her boarding the ship assisted by Terrance, and Vicky. They asked her if she wanted to press charges against Kevin, and she said no.

The short rings of the telephone on the desk interrupted her reflections on the whole incident. She reached for the phone, and then hesitated before picking it up. *What if it's Kevin? Did Terrance let him know my cabin number? What if he's calling to threaten me?* A couple more rings sounded. Anita picked up the phone, but didn't say anything. She waited for the caller to speak first. "Hello, hello." It was a man's voice. "Mrs. Roundtree, this is Security Officer Lopez. Hello, are you there?" Anita slowly exhaled and weakly said, "*Yes*, I'm here."

Officer Lopez asked if she was alone. She said yes. He proceeded. "Mrs. Roundtree we just wanted to update you on the current situation concerning Mr. Stephens. Anita felt a flash of embarrassment because she didn't even know the man's last name. Well without going into too much detail, Mr. Stephens is being detained in…, well, let's just say more secure quarters on the ship. He will be escorted off the ship under guard, in the morning when the ship docks. From there he will be in the hands of other authorities. We just wanted you to know you can feel free to move about the ship. You can go anywhere you want to go without concern of being bothered." "Thank you very much. I was concerned about venturing out of my cabin." "Well, we hope we have satisfied the current problem. If there is anything else we can do to make the remainder of your cruise safe and enjoyable, please don't hesitate to ask." "Thank you again Officer", she said. "You're very welcome Mrs. Roundtree. Enjoy your evening."

Anita placed the receiver back in its place, and breathed a sigh of relief. It was Christmas Eve, and she was going to get dressed and go out! The festive lights, music, and gayety of the holiday season would give her the pick-me-up she needed. As she was getting dressed, she vowed to stay out of the Bars and Clubs. She thought out loud; *"I may not be a Holy Roller, but I'm not stupid! I know it was Betty's prayer, and God's providence that brought me out of what could have been a disastrous mess. I think I'll sit in a nice Bistro, or go up to 'Breezes of the Sea' to experience the Christmas Eve evening without coming out of it looking like a drunken idiot!"*

# Chapter 20

The Captain's Christmas Ball was being held in the ship's other formal dining room; *'The Century'*. As Brandon and Beverly neared the area, photo stations were set up all throughout the corridors. Some were on the Lido deck, some on the Promenade; others outside the passageways between the elevators—and of course, adjacent to the dining room. You couldn't escape getting your picture taken. Beverly really wanted her picture taken in her semi-formal dress. She hadn't put it on so long, she was surprised it still fit.

After Ronald's death, there weren't many formal invitations that came her way—at least none that she cared to attend. She felt that Brandon wanted to have their picture taken too. When he came to escort her to the Ball, she was pleasantly surprised how strikingly handsome he looked in his tuxedo. Up until that time, she had only seen him in casual cruising attire.

Beverly was pondering over Brandon's appearance when the man behind the camera was beckoning them forward. He was saying, "Yes, you two are next." Beverly still wasn't sure if he was speaking to them, and pointed her finger toward herself. "Yes elegant lady. You and your handsome gentleman." Brandon leaned down to whisper in her ear, "I guess that means us", he said in a flattering tone of voice. The photographer positioned Beverly on a high stool, and instructed Brandon to stand behind her. Both of their faces must have shown a little tenseness, because the photographer encouraged them to relax; to loosen up and enjoy each other.

Beverly didn't know what Brandon was feeling, but she was feeling embarrassed. Brandon let his nervousness show when he was directed to hunch down and lean closer to Beverly's face. The man behind the camera kept saying things like; "Come on hubby, you can do better than that. She's not going to bite." When they thought he had taken enough shots, he surprised them by saying, "Now let me see that love you have for each other." A quick snap followed, and he said, "Now that's what I'm talking about! You folks just took a beautiful picture." Brandon helped Beverly down from the stool holding her hand in his to steady her maneuver from the stool to the floor. He continued to hold her hand, and he felt a boost of confidence as they neared *'The Century'* dining room.

The atmosphere was very festive, and the decorations were more than fabulous. Merry Christmas was on everyone's lips—well almost everyone. Some were saying 'Happy Holiday's', and some of the *old- timers* said 'Seasons Greetings'. A small line had begun to form leading into the dining room. It wasn't a long wait, and Beverly could see up ahead what the slight hold up was. Another photo station was set up along the side of the entry wall for those who wanted to get their picture taken with the Captain. We stopped to have our picture taken, and the photographer said the photos would be posted in the gallery by Christmas day after 2:00pm.

When they entered the room a live band was playing one of Beverly's favorite Christmas songs; *'Have Yourself a Merry Little Christmas'*. The Alto Saxophone made the instrumental music sound mellow and dreamy. Had she been at home, Beverly would have been singing out loud, and doing her little dance moves with the memory of Ronald in her arms. On the way to their assigned table, she spotted couples swaying back and forth in each other's arms on the dance floor. Then it hit her…*I'm at a Ball with a man. What if he asks me to dance?*

---

Kevin was as angry as a '*mad*' bull. The small cabin wasn't a jail cell, but there was no doubt that it was meant to separate and detain a person from the rest of the passengers. The room was very plain. It had a twin size bed, a cubbyhole closet, and no telephone. Kevin thought how funny it was that brochures always showed the exciting, luxurious side of taking a cruise, but he was one of the people who got to experience the flip side of the coin. He found out that the Captain and other Officers weren't there just for decorations, or for show. They were real ranking officers, with real authority.

Kevin knew he had messed up for sure this time. He called them every name in the book, now that he was behind closed doors. He was tempted to cause a big scene while being escorted to his new quarters, but the coward in him prodded through, and he didn't want any more charges added to the ones already pending.

*The punks,* he thought, *they even confiscated my cell phone.* A knock came on the door, and someone slid a paper under it. "Mr. Stephens, here's the room service menu. I'll be back around in about ten minutes to pick it up. Circle what you want and slide it back out under the door." Kevin looked the limited menu over. At least it offered a turkey dinner as one of its choices.

*Yeah, turkey; that's me! This was going to be a wasted Christmas Eve night. That Anita was an easy mark. Terrance and his noble, self-righteous self, had to interfere. Now, tonight is busted, and it looks like Christmas Day will be even worse. I can't even order a stinking drink. They took my ship-n-sail pass, and the cruise only serves alcohol in the clubs and dining rooms.*

Terrance was grateful that Kevin wasn't coming back to the room. He felt sorry for the guy. He really couldn't call him his *friend*. Maybe he was more of an acquaintance—a bad one. Terrance thought of the number of times he warned Kevin that one of these days his lifestyle was going to catch up with him. He reflected on his and Kevin's relationship. They were two men who were totally opposite of each other. He might have a drink every now and then, but Kevin was a very heavy drinker. He never used drugs–Kevin was a frequent user. He was not a *browser*. If he met a woman he thought he liked, he stuck with her until the both of them knew they were looking for the same thing, had the same goals. On the other hand, Kevin lied and cheated his way into most of his relationships just to get the woman in bed.  Terrance loved to go to church, and Kevin ran in the opposite direction.

Outside of those differences, the thing that puzzled Terrance was that no matter how many times he tried to distance himself from Kevin, he would eventually show up out of nowhere. It was always, "Hey buddy, where you been?" as if he had just seen him last week instead of last month. Theirs was surly a Yen Yang relationship, yet Terrance was sure he had an assignment to fulfill in this man's life; although he had no idea what it was.

_______________~_______________

The buffet units in 'Breezes of the Seas' were outstanding. Passengers tried to get as many pictures as they could of the marvelous ice sculpting's and food carvings before they were disturbed. The artistic designs of melons, meats, and ice carvings were extraordinary!

Vicky knew it would probably be nice, but she had no idea it would be this grand. She had no idea that food could be displayed so beautifully. If this was *that* up scaled in here, she could only imagine what the Captain's Ball must be like. Aside from the regular condiments on the tables, each table had an added Christmas centerpiece. Vicky excused herself from the table Terrance had chosen for them in order to take a few pictures of the buffet with her phone.

She really did it for an excuse to collect herself. Butterflies zipped back and forth in her stomach, and her mind was in a fog. Vicky knew that when she got panicky, her eyes got even larger; and she didn't need for that to happen. Actually the way Anita applied her eye makeup narrowed her eyes down a little. She kept telling herself to stay focused. She was used to being the side-kick, not the *main* attraction.

She took a few pictures, a couple of deep breathes, and headed back to her table. Terrance rose from his chair when he saw her approaching. She sat down and started to put her phone back in her back in her purse. "Hey, Terrance said, aren't you going to take my picture? I mean, I know the food looks good, but I think I clean up quite well too." He got out of his seat. "After all, this is our third; almost forth time together, if you count the encounter in the library, and I thought I was growing on you." Vicky felt embarrassed.

Terrance stood before her, and mimicked a magazine model's pose. She snapped the picture. But, before she could move to put her phone away, Terrance swooped in the seat next to her. "Oh no you don't. Now we need one together." He politely took her phone and clicked the button. Then he removed his phone from his inside jacket pocket, moved in closer to Vicky's face and clicked the button. The camera flashed before she could object.

Terrance went back to his seat across from Vicky. "Ya know, he said, these probably aren't going to be the best pictures in the world. The lighting is sort of dim in here. What say we stop by one of those professional photographer stations after dinner to have a pro take our picture?"

It had been so long since anyone had asked to purposely take a picture with her, Vicky didn't know how to respond. Whenever she was in a picture, it was because she was standing near Anita. That thought brought her mind back to her friend. *I wonder if Anita's doing okay?*

<h1 style="text-align:center">Chapter 21</h1>

The Ronald Sparks Sr. clan gathered for their traditional Christmas Eve celebration, except this year it was held at Emily and Wayne's house. The siblings were feeling the absence of their Mother, and as for their children, *their* grandmother. The grownups sent the kids to the den, while the ladies set things in order in the kitchen. RJ and Wayne strung the rest of the lights on the tree, and when that was done, they called in an order for take-out pizza for the kids. Things could have been going well for Beverly on the cruise, but Wayne and Emily had no way of knowing. Just in cast things didn't go so well for her; Wayne thought his wife ought to tell her brother and sister what she had done.

Emily was at her wits end anyway. She kept forgetting things. Her patients was seemingly short with people when the smallest detail didn't go according to her plan. Carol and Ronald Jr. knew it had to be more than Mom not being there for Christmas. Ronald asked his brother-in-law what was going on, and he told him he would have to ask his sister.

The main meal, and side dishes were finished and waiting. All that was left to do was to bake the sweet potato pie, frost the three layer coconut cake, and put the yeast rolls in the oven just before they sat down to eat. The pizza would arrive in a few minutes, giving the ladies time to take a break from the kitchen. If everything went smoothly, they would be sitting down to Christmas Eve dinner in about one hour. This gave Emily time to hold her confession conference with her siblings; and she was certain the kids would be hungry again by the time dinner was ready. Wayne volunteered to watch the kids while the others went up to the bedroom.

According to the calendar, it had only been two days, but for Emily's anguish, it seemed more like a week. She was certain her Mother had run into Melvin by now, but what she wasn't sure of was if her mother knew that she was behind the whole scheme. She hated to tell her brother and sister what she had done. Her guilty conscious was affecting her attitude, and disposition. She most likely had ruined her own mother's Christmas—no use ruining everybody else's.

Carol was appalled at what her sister told her. She couldn't believe that Emily would do such a thing; and then again she could believe that she could (*with her take-over attitude*). She accused her sister of being a *'busy-body'*, and a control freak. She was someone who thought she knew what was best for everybody. Carol was so upset, she threatened to go home. Wayne could hear that the siblings meeting had escalated to another level. Since the children were involved in pizza and "Frosty the Snow Man", he mounted the steps to his bedroom. He knew he needed to intervene before Christmas got out of hand.

Wayne didn't want to appear that he was defending his wife, because he wasn't. Emily told them that she had already received a severe scolding from her husband, and all she wanted to do was to let them know how sorry she was, and why she was in such a disgruntle mood. She apologized and asked for their forgiveness.

RJ wanted to forgive his sister, but he did it with an ultimatum— that she would promise to mend her ways. Emily agreed, and he crossed the bedroom floor to give her a hug. However, it wasn't going to be so easy with Carol. She wanted to forgive her sister, and even though she said the words, she knew the emptiness of the confession would have to take hold in her heart.

Ronald said he was going for a walk to clear his head. When he opened the door, aromas from the kitchen seeped into their nostrils. The sisters, pushing their emotions aside, dashed down the stairs to rescue the nearly scorched pies.

---

The 'Century' dining room was breathtaking! It didn't have the long oblong tables like 'Breezes of the Seas'. The tables were round, and could seat up to eight people per table. Beverly guess that made for a cozier, more intimate atmosphere. The room had two areas of seating on each side, and one larger area across the back loaning itself to a 'U-shaped' dinning space.

The band sat midway the room, and a cleared area for dancing was set up in front of them. The center pieces on each table held a lighted candle surrounded by a holly and ivy Christmas ring. There was an elegantly flocked Christmas tree near the front of the dining room, surrounded with beautifully wrapped boxes with bows. A photographer was standing by for those who wanted to get their picture taken near the tree. The ornaments and lights were spectacular!

A little gift box was set at each of the place settings. It made you feel like it was already Christmas. Inside each of the boxes was a keepsake tree ornament with the ship's name, and date engraved on it. *Wow,* Beverly thought. *A free gift. I didn't expect that.* A special meal just for the affair was prepared by the head chef. There were two choices on the menu.

MENU #1

Grapefruit Grenadine
Roast Turkey  –  Oyster Stuffing
Twice baked Potatoes    Gravy
Herbed Green Beans
Rutabaga and Apple Bake
Tutti Fruitcake - Chocolate hazelnut plum pudding

MENU #2

Cranberry Shrimp Ceviche Cups
Fresco Cheese Crustier with Pumpkin Mojo
Teriyaki Glazed Salmon – Spring Onion Rice
Roasted pepper Cornbread Stuffing
Butternut Squash – Baked w/Cranberry
Oatmeal Crumble
Orange Meringue Pie

Each table was served and replenished with a platter of international crackers and flavored cheeseballs, grapes, assortments of sliced cheeses, and fresh baked rolls. Beverly surmised the *topper* that paid for the meal ticket was the free champagne, and imported wine. A basket was on each table that had small strips of blank paper in it and a pen. This was for anyone who had special request for the band.

———————⁓———————

Melvin and Betty followed the Maitra D' into the beautifully decorated Ballroom. All the decorations were so oversized. Not like the ones you use in your home, but more like what you see at the Mall, or in an upscale mansion. Melvin and Betty passed several tables on the left side of the room, and the Maitra D' stopped at a round table just steps from the space reserved for dancing. Their names were on place cards next to each other on the side of the table facing the entryway. Betty felt a little nervous, but was honored that Melvin not only paid for the tickets, but made sure they were seated beside each other.

Melvin waited while the Maitra D' held the chair out for Betty, and when she was seated, he took his own. Greetings and introductions moved around the table. A few of the faces he recognized, having seen them at other times around the ship. Melvin shared that he and Betty were old schoolmates who hadn't seen each other for nearly thirty years, and accidently bumped into each other on this cruise.

He, Betty and two other people at the table were first time cruisers. One elderly couple, maybe close to their eighties, said they only had one adult child who never married, so they had no grandchildren, or other family. Their son lived out of the country most of the time, so they took their first Christmas cruise about ten years ago, and they have been doing it ever since. The other pair was two sisters who decided to come on the holiday cruise to enjoy all the amenities they couldn't afford to have at home. They also wanted to escape the cold weather and snow for a week or so, even though they knew they would have to face it when they got back—but at least they would have warm memories to cuddle up to.

Betty and Melvin decided that each of them would order different menu selections that way, she could share pictures of both of their meals when she got back home. Melvin partook of the hors d'oeuvres and fresh baked Christmas breads and Stolen. His eyes wandered around the softly lit room, and suddenly rested on a lady sitting at a table two sections down from his. It was Beverly!

He knew he would probably run into her again before the cruise was over, but he didn't expect this. She was ravishing! Her hair was pulled up on each side of her face in soft curls, and he could see when she turned slightly to whisper something to Brandon that she left a portion of the back of her tresses fall freely to its full length. Her shoulders were almost bare except for the thin spaghetti straps that held up the dress around her bosom. He thought to himself, *I don't think I've ever seen her bare shoulders before'*. At that precise moment Beverly looked up to find Melvin staring directly at her. She was surprised to find that she was still somewhat agitated with what went down, although she said she forgave him; *or at least she thought she had.*

Melvin consciously shook himself, and drew his attention back to Betty. He could only hope that she didn't notice him gawking at Beverly because he had really been drawn to Betty these last few days. *He needed to convince himself it wasn't just because Beverly rejected him.* He looked up just as their server was approaching the table with their soup and shrimp cocktail appetizers.

Betty nudged him. "Hey Melvin, I believe that man is trying to get your attention." She pointed toward Brandon and Beverly's table. "Do you know that couple?" *What am I going do now? This could end up being a big mess.* Brandon was giving him a friendly wave, so he waved back. Beverly managed a slight smile, and he gave a gentlemanly nod of the head back to her. Melvin cleared his throat. "Um, yes." And making sure he mentioned the man's name first he said, "The man is Brandon, and the lady's name is Beverly. Actually, she's from my hometown (he didn't want to lie). We bumped into each other yesterday and she introduced me to Brandon. They met right here on this cruise." "Well, like people always say, Betty retorted, it's a small world, and it gets smaller every day. You never know who you will run into; look at us." "You're right about that", Melvin said.

Finally the unexpected that Beverly feared happened. Brandon asked her if she cared to take a spin around the floor with him. That was his way of asking her for a dance. She thought to herself, *why didn't I practice a few dance steps around the house before I left?* She answered her own question immediately…*because you never expected to meet a gentleman who would ask you to dance.* Aside from the 'Welcome Aboard' party on Tuesday, dancing was not one of the things she planned on doing. It certainly wasn't planned for then, or now.

The server said they had about ten minutes before the entrée would be served, so if they wanted to get a dance in they had enough time. Beverly was surprised that Brandon was a dancing man. Some things you kind of pick up on just from being around a person, and she didn't pick that up about him at all. She really hadn't danced *that* way since she use to be in Ronald's arms.

Beverly accommodated him with a gentle smile, but she didn't say no. Brandon rose from his chair and stood behind hers. She pushed her seat back and rose halfway to a standing position. Brandon reached for her arm to assist in her standing. Now that they were walking to the dance floor, Brandon wasn't sure why he asked Beverly to dance. He hadn't danced in years. Maybe it was the atmosphere, maybe it was the music—maybe *both.* He thought, *this is crazy!* And just then another thought came to his mind. It was the way that Gracie made him feel; *like he could do anything.* Yes, that's the way he was beginning to feel when he was around Beverly…like he could do anything!

By the time they reached the dance floor area, the tempo of the music picked up. *'Whew!' He whispered a prayer. Thank you Lord.* He just didn't know that Beverly had whispered the same one.

# Chapter 22

The evening was extraordinary, and the ship's photographers were taking full advantage of every shot they could get. They were taking pictures of the groups at each table, couples at the table and those on the dance floor. It can be quite embarrassing when you think you are photographing a couple, and you got it all wrong. That's what happened at the table across from them. One of the wives excused herself to go to the restroom, and when the photographer got to that table he kept trying to get the man (her husband) to move in closer to the woman seated on the other side of him.

Not clear on what the photographer was trying to capture, he only leaned in a little. When her husband, or whoever the man was who had come with that particular lady realized what was happening, he scooted closer to her and put his arm around her shoulder. He must have made a funny comment, because the group at the table erupted in laughter, and the photographer began to apologize profusely.

Brandon and Beverly had a good laughing at each other too. They were trying their hand at doing the "Bop" (a regular fast pace dance style popular from the late 40's through the early 60's). Swinging her around with one extended arm, and catching her hand in his, Brandon said, (in a capricious tone of voice) "You do know that I don't know what I'm doing, don't you?" Beverly replied over the noise of the band, "That's all right, neither do I." They both laughed again. The song ended, and they were headed off the dance floor when the band immediately started playing "The Christmas Song"; better known as '*Chestnuts Roasting on an Open Fire*'. Brandon stopped in his tracts. He looked Beverly in the eyes, and said, "Do you mind?" It was his way of asking her to stay and dance this dance with him. She put her hand in his and said, "It would be my pleasure."

Beverly was as nervous as she had ever been. She was bewildered and uncertain of why she said yes. The pace was slower, but the style of dancing it called for was *closer*. No man had held her this close since her husband had passed away. Before she could think, she was already in Brandon's arms swaying back and forth to the music. *She dare not allow herself to get too familiar with this man. She dare not allow herself to be drawn to close in his embrace.* Was her cold, lonely, wintery heart giving way to the warmth of knowing that someone could care for her again in *that* way? Was her *uncertain heart* moving forward without her permission, or had she relinquished it the first day of their meeting?

Betty told herself she wasn't about to become jealous over a woman she didn't know; nor was she about to become resentful to a man *for all intents and purposes*, she'd just met. After all, she hadn't seen Melvin for almost thirty years. What did she know about his adult life? Nothing! She decided to ignore the way she saw him look at the lady he knew from his home town; whomever *she* was. But, she could tell one thing for dog-gone-sure, and that was that the lady was more than a casual acquaintance he just happened to bump into. *'Forget it!'* She thought. *Come to think of it, there's not much he knows about me either. Anyway, its Christmas time, I'm on a cruise where I expected to be sitting with two other women; instead, I'm on a date, with a handsome guy at a Ball and having a great time. So what if we never see each other again after this is over…at least we have tonight!*
When she looked up, Melvin was gazing at her with a smile on his face. "What is it? Betty said, why are you looking at me with that funny look on your face?" "Oh, for one reason in particular. It's because that's the look you used to have on your face every now and then back in high school. You know, like when you were far, far away…you were somewhere else, not sitting in class with the rest of us. Hey, you hardly touched your appetizer. Didn't you care for it?" "Oh no—I mean yes. It taste

wonderful. It's just that I got a little distracted for a minute." Betty was slightly embarrassed, but more amazed at what Melvin said...*just like she used to do in high school.*

---

Vicky tried to be relaxed, but clearly this was a situation she was not used to. She had gotten so use to playing '*second fiddle*' to Anita, and to any other friends she socialized with, she felt like a duck out of water. Terrance was giving her first-hand attention. She questioned if she should keep her guard up, or if to lower her defenses a little. Vicky didn't sense that he was anything like his friend Kevin, and that's why their relationship seemed so odd to her.

She needed a few moments alone to think. She excused herself to refill her coffee cup with hot apple cider. Terrance offered to get it for her, but she made an excuse of also wanting to peruse the Buffet tables again. She actually wanted to whisper a prayer in the hopes that this man was not out to trick her–that *was* if God still heard her prayers. At one time she was very active in the church, but after her divorce she hooked up with Anita, and started to run the streets again. The more she went *clubbing*, the more she distanced herself from her church friend, and the church.

Terrance dabbled at the food on his plate. *"Okay* he said to himself, *what's going on here? Are you really interested in this woman, or are you just stringing her along? You'd better decide how you feel about her?"* He chuckled to himself. He didn't know why, but there was something about Vicky that interested him. Sure, there were some cosmetic features that could stand a little adjustments, but everybody had something they didn't like about themselves. His was his feet. They started growing during puberty, and seemly never stopped. Of course most people aren't drawn to a person's feet when they first meet them. Even though he was only an average of 5'10.5", he usually stretched his height saying he was six feet whenever anyone asked. He was very conscious of his size fourteen shoe. For a basketball player that would be normal, but for a pigeon-toed attorney, he was timidly self-conscious.

From the few occasions they had been out together, Terrance could tell that Vicky liked jewelry. He was glad that the gift he picked out for her was jewelry. The pieces were a matching set, but he wanted to give them to her as separate gifts. He planned to give her the necklace tonight, and the matching bracelet tomorrow *for Christmas.* The sterling silver set wasn't large and bulky. The chain necklace had a small Bible pendant attached to it. It was delicate and nice; not over powering. The matching piece was a charm bracelet. The sterling silver charms on it were a Bible, a dove, a cross, and a heart. He liked it.

It had been a while since he'd bought a present for any female except for his mother, his sister, and his niece. Terrance thought about his brief engagement to Darlene, and the hurt he felt afterwards. He knew about the pain of a broken heart. He almost made it to the altar, but his fiancée broke off their engagement. She evidently wanted more than he could offer her at that time. He was in a financial struggle for a short period, and things got a little tight, but he was glad he stuck with his plan. From that point on, he was very careful with relationships. If he was to be honest with himself— he avoided them. He finished Law school, passed the Bar, and *now* he was getting along quite well.

Terrance patted his jacket pocket again to reassure himself he remembered to bring the small box. He was trying to decide the best time to give the necklace to Vicky. On her way back, Vicky slowed her pace to look at the handsome man sitting at her table, and a sudden sadness came over her. A voice in her head she tried to ignore, pushed through to her moment of joy. *Don't get your hopes up honey, because when this ship docks in Miami, it'll all be over!*

Terrance stood when Vicky approached the table. She sat and took a few sips from her cup.

"Now that you're back, Terrance said, I think I'll pay a visit to the dessert bars for some of those delicious, tantalizing delicacies! He raised his eyebrows, and widened his smile as if to say, how did you like those adjectives? Can I get you anything?" Vicky whispered a *"No thank you"*. She really wanted to try one of those double chocolate fudge brownies that were laced with crushed candy cane chips, but she was being very conscious of having any food particles or leftovers clinging to the uneven crevices in her teeth.

Vicky sat gazing around the spacious setting to see not only family gatherings, but also couples. Her mind floated to Betty and her gentleman friend. She could only try to imagine how beautiful the decorations must be at the Captain's Christmas Eve Ball. She hoped Betty would think to take a few pictures so she and Anita could share in the excitement of it all; although she wasn't quite sure how excited Anita would be.

Terrance maneuvered his way through the somewhat crowed dining area back to the table. He was carrying two plates of food that held an array of desserts, fancy cheeses and mixed grapes, little tarts, and classic holiday *Divinities* of mini *Petit Fours*. He placed the dishes on the table. "What in the world!" exclaimed Vicky? "Now, now, don't get excited", Terrance hurriedly said in defense of the overload of delicacies, "I have a plan. You see, this is a *Now-or-Later* plate. "A what?" Vicky asked. Terrance's effort to explain the pile of food, along with the expression on his face made Vicky smile.

"Well, you see, we'll eat this, that, and *those* now. He was pointing randomly at nothing in particular on the plates, and we'll save the rest for later. I know how particular some of you ladies can be about keeping your figures intact, and by the way–you have nothing to worry about. Yours looks smashing in that dress, so I thought we could eat little pinches at a time while we finish our date."

Vicky thought, *this man is really flirting with me…not my friend, but with me.* She smiled outwardly at his humor, but inwardly her heart was franticly pumping. She didn't let the compliment he said about her figure slip by either.

# Chapter 23

Anita strolled around the Lido deck pretending she was on her way to meet someone; when actually there was no one to meet. If it was this difficult to try and fool herself, she was sure she couldn't fool anybody else. She wasn't about to keep up this charade all night. She thought she'd better stop while she was ahead mainly because she didn't want to pass the same group of people two times. *If this didn't beat all,* she thought, *my two friends out on dates, and me; Anita Roundtree without a man.* She slowed her pace, and decided to sit in one of the open lounge areas. Talking to herself out loud she said, "This has to be 'pay-back' for all the nasty things I said to my husband before I left for the cruise."

Her husband was the one who was trying to hang onto the marriage, not her. Anita did every despicable thing she could think of to try and get him to divorce her. He even wanted them to go to marriage counseling together, but she refused. Anita didn't want counseling. She wanted her freedom, and she wanted his money!

She blamed those *church* people and his mother for filling his head with all that '*righteous*' and honorable husband stuff. Anita had been cheating on him for the past year or so, and the fool was still hoping things will turn around—or at least hoping that she would turn around. Anita was mean enough to make a joke of it, telling her husband he could come along on the cruise if he wanted to, but I knew his answer would be *no*. He said, "What's the use in going on a romantic cruise if the romance is one sided?"

Anita's blood boiled every time she thought about the way she was tricked. She was usually the one who called the shots on her *private* escapades. She would go to a club, get the guy to buy her a few drinks, do some provocative dancing or slow grinding with him, and if she wanted to go farther with him, she would—otherwise she'd use the excuse of being a married woman and she was afraid her husband was following her, and she didn't want to cause the guy any trouble. Of course the guy would be angry as all get out, but she didn't care. She had a good time, and would probably never see him again.

The only problem was that, that scheme didn't work on a cruise ship. Anita was sure what she wanted to do. Everywhere she looked people were paired up together, or in family groups. She could see that most of the people weren't hanging around just doing *nothing*. She felt out of place. The rumbling in her stomach started again. She was way past hungry, but she didn't want to go somewhere and sit all alone. Things had not worked out the way she thought they would have. Maybe this Christmas cruise was not such a good idea—at least not for her…a married woman running away from a life she despised. She decided to go back to the cabin and order from the room service menu.

———————～———————

The dining experience for the Captain's Christmas Eve Ball was superb! No minor detail was left unattended to. The climax of the evening ended with the Captain presenting his officers. Then, sounds of delight eroded from the audience as each one of the male officers strolled through the dining room to select a lady to take a spin with him on the dance floor. After that, the serving staff and Maître D's sang "Have Yourself a Merry Little Christmas" while they placed a clear, cellophane gift bag in front of each person. Some of them were fastened with red bows, and the others with gold. The bag held beautifully decorated Marzipans, melt-in-your mouth Truffles, and white chocolate fudge with pecans. Beverly thought, *this is the end to a perfect evening.* But she was still looking for an opportunity to give Brandon his gift.

Those families who had smaller children with them began to leave out right away. According to the daily events newsletter, there was going to be a reading of "*The Night Before Christmas*" by Santa

Clause in the Youth Activity room. After the reading, the children would receive a gift from the jolly old elf himself. This (of course) was prearranged with the Cruise director, and the parents. Unbeknownst to the kids, the parent who wanted their child (or children) to be in on this special happening, brought a wrapped gift with the child's first and last name on it to the director of the event. So no child would be left out, extra gifts were on hand for boys and girls from the ages of three to ten years old.

The band continued to play while the tables were being cleared, and a few couples seized the opportunity to get in one last dance before leaving the Ball. Others made their way to the huge Christmas tree and the photographers. Melvin asked Betty if they could take a picture together in front of the tree. She said she didn't mind, but thought of the many pictures that had already been taken during dinner. She tried not to be so negative, but she didn't understand what was going on. Melvin saw the hesitant look on her face, but he didn't want to ruin the other part of his surprise gift.

He wanted a picture of just the two of them together without the distractions going on around them; like other diners and the waiters. He had purchased an 8"x10" picture frame while in the gift shop, because he wanted to give Betty a memoir photo of the two of them. He knew he had to wait until Christmas day to get it from the photo gallery. He could only hope he wasn't being to forward in his assumptions. Betty took her compact mirror from her evening bag and applied fresh lipstick. She took a quick peek at her teeth, and brushed a loose lock of hair back in place.

Melvin looked at Betty through admiring eyes. Something about her made him feel good about himself. It wasn't the same as he thought he felt about Beverly, because no matter how many times he tried to convince himself he was in love with her, he always came away with a guilty conscious to deal with. He had to think about what he was moving into with Betty. He knew he was probably moving it along too quickly. He wasn't sure how to pursue this relationship, or even if it was one that Betty wanted.

Was he being drawn to this woman because of his failure with Beverly? Had he really been in love with Bev, or was it because she possessed the many virtues lacking in his ex-wife? A little voice inside his head said, *whatever you decide, you'd better decide it in a hurry, because it will affect more than just your life!* Melvin knew it was a cowardly fear that came over him. *No*! He almost said out loud. *I will not be cheated out of happiness again!*

———————— ～ ————————

Brandon and Beverly came out of the dining room and stepped to the balcony railing overlooking the 'Atrium'. Brandon was still trying to figure out a way to give Beverly his Christmas gift. He just couldn't pull the perfume out of his pocket, and say "Here, I got you something." No, that wouldn't do.

This is where he needed his creativity to kick in. Romantic thoughts he presumed dead and gone, begun to stir in his mind. While standing there, Beverly thanked him again for a lovely evening.

The play they went to didn't cost them anything. The stage plays were part of the entertainment packages that came with the purchase of the cruise ticket, but the tickets for the Ball were an extra expense. Just like purchasing one of the excursion packages, they were a little pricy. She knew that because the *event* was listed in the cruise's daily newsletter. Not only that, he rented a Tuxedo. That could not have been cheap either.

Brandon's voice interrupted her musing. "You know Beverly, the night's still young." He nodded his head toward the open Atrium area below. "Would you like to sit for a while and enjoy the scenery and music?"

The music was the same background music being piped throughout the ship. Beverly surmised most of the live orchestras and bands were being used in different venues for the evening. She said she would love to sit and relax for a while. She was glad he asked, because that would give them a more private setting where she could give him the gift she had for him. They went down in the elevator, and Brandon reached over to hold her hand. It seemed like a stream of excitement floated from his hand to encapsulate her entire body. She fought to maintain her steadiness. When the elevator doors opened her knees wobbled. Beverly pleasantly asked for him to find a nice place for them to sit while she went to powder her nose.

Brandon looked around and found a small vacant booth. The table was just inside the semi-circle area designed around the center stage which was the center attraction between the elaborate staircases on both sides.

The booth was almost directly in front of the enchanting winter wonderland scene set up on the platform. The trees had presents around them, and the lights created the perfect ambiance for what he had in mind—a more private setting to give Beverly her present.


Brandon waved his hand in the air when he saw Beverly enter the Atrium. The horseshoe-shaped tufted bench gave an open, yet reclusive feel to their seating. Beverly scooted into the seat and moved close to Brandon. He was a little surprised, but delighted!

The two of them sat admiring the scenery while the spirit of Christmas filled their hearts. They found out more about each other's life, and talked about how nice the cruise was. They shared that neither one of them knew what to expect *as this was their first Christmas cruise*. Beverly had been on a water boat cruise before, but this was Brandon's first time ever on any type of cruise. She said she expected the holiday cruise to be nice, but she never expected anything like this.

Brandon took advantage of her last statement to interject the wording he was looking for in lieu of the occasion. "And my lovely lady, one of the things I didn't expect was to meet such a beautiful, charming lady as yourself. So, on that note I would like to say how much I have enjoyed your company, and this cruise." He reached in his coat pocket and pulled out the rectangular wrapped box. "Merry Christmas Beverly."

She was stunned—thrown for a loop!  Her face lit up with the joy of a child receiving a much wished for gift from Santa. Her voice pushed through the lump forming in her throat. "Thank you so much. You've already been so kind, so generous, you didn't have to get me a present too." Brandon tore himself away from the watery glaze forming in her eyes. "Believe me, it was my pleasure." Smiling fondly, Beverly reached in her evening bag and brought out a small package topped with a purple and silver bow. She presented it to Brandon saying, "Merry Christmas Mr. Woods. You'll never know

how enjoyable you've made this Christmas for me."
This time it was Brandon who was surprised.
"What? Are you kidding me? Now this is really a
surprise."

"Well, should we open our gifts now,
Beverly said, or wait until tomorrow?" "Let's make
it a compromise, he said, we'll sit and listen to
more Christmas music for a while, and we'll open
our gifts before we close out the evening."
"Agreed", Beverly said, "but only on one account."
Brandon gave her a questioning look with a raise of
his eyebrow. Beverly snickered and said, "Only if
you promise to sing along, with a song or two
before we leave. You have such a wonderful
voice."

She moved in a little closer to him. Brandon,
knowing she wouldn't mind lifted his arm and put it
around her shoulders saying, "In light of the present
company, how can I refuse."
A certain figure of a young man stood at the
balcony railing directly above them, and a pleasant
smile donned his face. "Merry Christmas Pops", he
said in a whisper.

# Chapter 24

Vicky could not pinpoint the instant she became aware of her feelings, but somewhere during their date her confidence began to take an upward swing over her normal feelings of low self-esteem. She couldn't remember the last time she had a conversation with a man when he wasn't looking over her shoulder at a prettier woman nearby. Talking with Terrance was easy. He was interested in what she had to say; or at least he pretended to be.

Around about now Vicky's stomach was past full. She glanced at the near empty plates on the table and realized there wasn't much left of what Terrance called '*the later*'. It seemed the more they talked, the more they nibbled. All of a sudden she blurted out, "Look Terrance. This has got to stop! We've got to go. I have to get up from this table that is, if I'm able to move. I must have eaten close to ten thousand calories just in the last hour."

Terrance had to chuckle at that, because he thought something terrible had happened. "I didn't mean to laugh, but I didn't know what had happened." His smile was enough to make Vicky laugh. "Okay, he said, you caught me in the very act. I confess. You see, I was trying to keep the conversation going with you for as long as I could. I just wanted this date to last longer." He paused for a few seconds. "But, let's say you don't count calories for the rest of the cruise. It's Christmas! So, I'll tell you what I'm willing to do. He paused for a moment. I'll be your calorie counting guard if you promise to save your days, afternoons, and evenings for me. That way both of us can watch your figure together."

Thoughts began to toss around in Vicky's head. *I may be out of practice with this dating thing, but I'm not slow! Not only is this man doing some serious flirting, but I think he just asked to see me for the remainder of the cruise.* A warning flag went up in Vicky's spirit, but this time it wasn't *Red*, or *Orange*. It had mellowed down to *Yellow*. None the less, a flag was still there, though not strong enough to make her want to turn down his offer. "Oh boy! Terrance said. This doesn't look good. I guess I came at you full throttle with that one. I apologize. Sometimes my mouth says what my mind is thinking before I can stop it. I'll understand if you have to think it over. Occasionally my attorney bluntness can get in the way of my *savoir-faire* smoothness." That was *such* a corny lie. He saw a smirk rise on Vicky's face, and he had to laugh about it himself.

Terrance fished in his pocket for the little box. "Well, corny or not, just to prove how sincere I am, I'd like to say *Merry Christmas*. You've been really great about this whole escapade concerning Kevin, and I hope you'll consider seeing me again." Vicky was floored! The last time a man gave her anything; it was divorce papers. "Go ahead, open it".

Vicky opened the box and stared down at the gorgeous pendent and chain. She didn't know what to say. Terrance was so excited, he couldn't wait for her to try it on. It had been ages since he'd brought a gift for a lady, let alone jewelry. "Can I see it on you?" Everything seemed to moving in slow motion for Vicky, like the moment was moving her along in a cloud. She fumbled several times trying to undo the clasp on the necklace she was wearing, and before she realized what was happening, Terrance was standing behind her to assist her in her effort. He probably was unaware of what the touch of his hands on the back of her neck was doing to her. Vicky's body shivered. Terrance apologized saying something about his cold hands, but Vicky knew differently. He may have thought his hands were cold, but they sent sweltering electrodes throughout her body.

Since he was already standing behind her, Terrance asked if she needed help with the chain he had just given her. Vicky's pulse rose against her temples. She could barely whisper a '*yes*'. Stretching both of his arms down across her shoulders to reach for the gift on the table, he lifted the necklace from the box, and fastened it around her neck. This time Terrance trembled. The scent of

Vicky's perfumed hair, his brush against her soft shoulders and touching the nape of her neck nearly enfeebled the sturdy courtroom attorney.

———————〜———————

Melvin couldn't deny that he had a warning in his spirit not to tamper with this lady's life if he wasn't serious about his feeling for her. The problem was, he wasn't sure how he felt. He *did* know that he had made an awful mistake with his feelings for Beverly, but it's impossible to adore someone for over five years, and then drop those feelings overnight. He also admitted to himself that he had a strong attraction toward Betty. He didn't want this to be a 'ship to shore' romance, but he also didn't want to move it along too quickly just because he knew Beverly had met someone else. He didn't want his feelings of jealously, anger, and embarrassment to color his sentiments toward Betty, because he really did enjoy her company.

On their way out they stopped to pose for a photo. Melvin wanted one of them standing in front of the tree, not sitting on a stool. He felt somewhat deceitful about wanting them to stand, but he knew when he got home, he wanted to view *all* of Betty; not just from the waist up. He was out of practice when it came to the dating thing, so he decided to ask Betty what she wanted to do—*and he hoped she didn't want to call it a night.* Betty said she wasn't sure, but there must be something else to do for the evening. *Well, that doesn't get me off the hook,* he thought, *but at least it let me know she wasn't ready to turn in for the night.*

"Well, let's say we take a stroll around the ship, and take in the sights and sounds of the season. There must be other Christmas stuff going on tonight that we can do, but I don't want to bore you." "Oh, I don't know, she said, I've had a pretty exciting evening so far, so I'll just keep following your lead." Betty slipped her arm around Melvin's elbow, and his confidence level rose about ten degrees.

They walked for another ten to fifteen minutes. Finally Betty confessed that her heels were killing her. They were cute, for dress-up, but now they were hurting her feet. She braced herself against Melvin's side, and removed her heels. He could have kicked himself for suggesting a long walk. It didn't cross his mind that she was wearing high heels, and he (of course) was wearing flat shoes. He was enjoying the evening so much, he wanted it to last as long as it could, but he asked. "Do you think you have to go back to your cabin?" "No way!" Betty exclaimed. That is unless you don't care to walk around the ship with a woman in her bare feet." But, I thought you were afraid you might ruin…" Before he could finish his statement, Betty finished it for him. "What, my stockings?" She raised her left leg, and wiggled her bare toes in the air. "Nope, see… no stockings."

Melvin could tell Betty had no idea how exciting a woman's bare legs and wiggling toes could be to a red-blooded American man. He maintained his cool, and chalked it up to her being out of touch with the opposite sex. But Melvin had to confess to himself, *maybe, at this juncture anything can turn me on.*

They ended up in one of the ship's alcoves located between on board shops and venues. The soft background music they heard throughout the ship seemed to increase in volume. Melvin took a few steps over to one of the posted marquees. "Well. Look-a-here. We're in luck. This says there's something going on in the Palace Theatre. Betty read the marquee. "Hum, The Sights and Sounds of Christmas *(with music to photographic accompaniment).* That sounds perfect", she said.

They entered the plush theatre, adjusting their eyes to the dim lighting. Melvin chose one of the semi-circle booths near the rear of the theatre. He didn't want Betty to walk too far in her bare feet. The theatre was just the setting he needed. It set the atmosphere for good *gift giving.* They sat quietly for several minutes enjoying the dimly lit theatre, the Christmas music, and nostalgic scenes that seemed to hold found memories for both of them. Melvin brought his arm up to rest around Betty's shoulders, and asked if she was enjoying the evening. She drew her legs up on the cushioned bench bending her knees so her legs rested on the velvety surface.

"Comfy?" Melvin asked. She nodded her head *'yes'* saying, "Now all we need is cracking logs in a fireplace, and a plate of Christmas cookies." "Who knows, he said, maybe a picture will flash across the screen for us."  He pulled the small wrapped package from his pocket, and placed it on the table. "Merry Christmas Betty, and thank you for saving me from myself." She had no idea what he meant by that statement, and her face must have shown it. Melvin didn't want the evening to be spoiled, so he said, "Never mind about what I just said, I'll explain it to you later." *And then again, he thought...maybe I won't.* Betty's face showed the delight of a lady on Christmas morning getting a wonderfully unexpected surprise. "These are beautiful. I don't know what to say." She leaned over and gave Melvin a quick peck on the cheek. "Yes I do, Thank you. Thank you very much."

<hr>

Anita moped back to the cabin feeling sorrier for herself than she had ever felt before. She knew she had only herself to blame. Sooner or later her egotistical, arrogant ways had to catch up with her. She sat at the vanity to dial room service. *How could things have gone so wrong?* Anita looked at her reflection in the mirror. Her eyes had already begun to swell with tears. *You're not so smart now, are you? Look at yourself. You're ruining your life, and everyone else's around you.*

The tears overflowed her eyelids and trickled down her cheeks, causing her mascara to run. She let the black liquid flow with her tears. Her nose began to run, and she reached to the back of the vanity, and grabbed a few tissues out of the opened box. She wiped her eyes, and her dripping nose. Looking at the woman in the mirror didn't give her such a high and lofty opinion of Mrs. Anita Roundtree. *Mrs. Anita Roundtree. That's right!* The non-speaking voice said back to her. *You're a married woman with a husband back home who loves you.*

Anita began to sob uncontrollably. She had to get a hold of herself. She ran into the bathroom and splashed cold water on her face. While she was there she decided to wash her makeup off. She felt a twinge of hunger, so she went to the phone to place her order. She wanted to shower and change into her PJ's, but because so many passengers were out for the evening, the galley said her order would only take between fifteen to twenty minutes.

She went to her purse to get a tip for the steward who would bring up her tray. Anita sat on the edge of the bed hoping her eyes weren't too puffy and red from crying. A sudden thought entered her mind. *I think I'll call my husband when we dock in Puerto Rico. Who knows, I might even try to get a flight home.*

# Chapter 25

Vicky touched the little Bible locket around her neck. She could hardly believe that someone thought enough of her to buy her a gift. This was something she never expected. Sure, men have been courteous to her when she was with Anita—and come to think of it, some not so courteous, but to have a gentleman buy something for her just because…well just because he liked her had not happened in a long, long time. Vicky apologized to Terrance for not having a present for him. She didn't go as far as to say; *because she never expected for him to hang around her that long without double dating with Anita and Kevin.*

Terrance told her that was okay with him; that he didn't give her the gift in order to get one back. As soon as he said that, and idea popped into his head. "But, he said, you can give me something I've been waiting for." Vicky's defenses flared up. *Oh boy, I knew this was too good to be true!* Terrance continued on with what he was saying. He pulled out his phone, and said, "Let's say we take a *selfie* together with you wearing your beautiful Christmas locket, and then you can give me your contact information so I can text, or email the picture to you." He knew it was a lame way of asking for her phone number and email address, but maybe if he had said it quick enough, he was hoping she wouldn't notice.

He pulled the vacant chair out on Vicky's side of the table up close to hers, and sat in it before she could object to his suggestion. He leaned in, and extended his right arm out as far as he could. He put his left arm around Vicky's shoulder, and said, "Say Christmas." They looked at the picture, and it was somewhat blurred. That may have been because Terrance's hand was shaking. Vicky wanted to see the picture because she never takes close-ups because of her overly defined features. Although the picture was blurry, she noticed that her protruding teeth did not show as much as she thought they would have. *Maybe,* she thought, *it was because they said 'Christmas'*, instead of *'smile'*, or *'cheese'* causing her lips to close in tighter around her teeth. Whatever the reason, she had more confidence in posing for the second shot.

Vicky gave Terrance the contact information he desired. She figured, *'What the heck'! It's not like he's actually going to call me.* She didn't want to end up disappointed over something that may never come about. Terrance said he wanted to find out where security was holding Kevin. He wanted to see if they would let him speak to Kevin before they deported him in the morning. Vicky was ready to turn in for the night. Terrance walked her back to her cabin. They both commented on how much they enjoyed the evening. When they reached her cabin, Vicky removed the room card from her purse.

"Here, let me do that for you", Terrance said. She put the card in his hand, but instead of slipping it in the key slot, he held it up in the air. "Come to think of it, he said, there is one more thing that I request of you before I let you say goodnight, (he moved in closer to Vicky) that is that you will promise to have Christmas breakfast with me in the morning." Vicky was relieved! "Okay", she said, and deciding to put a little whit in the situation said, providing I can get one more thing from you." "What's that?" "Your last name, she said shyly. It's a little quirk of mine. I never go on a second date with a guy unless I know his last name."

Terrance used his free hand to reach for Vicky's. "It's Weber; Terrance K. Weber!" Her voice came out in a whisper.

"What does the *K* stand for?" Terrance leaned down to her face and gently brushed her lips with his own. "Kiss, he said, 'K' stands for a good night *kiss*." He placed the card in the key slot, and pushed down on the handle when the green light came on. Anita was sitting at the small round table drinking something from a coffee mug. He peeped in the room to ask how she was feeling. Rather than divulge her true feelings, she just said "*Better, much better*". Terrance put the card back in Vicky's hand. He moved to one side to allow Vicky to enter the room. He gave her a wink of his eye, and a smug smile saying, "And I'll see you young lady in the morning."

He turned and strutted down the corridor intending to make a few phone calls to inquire about Kevin before going to bed.

Vicky just stood there in the doorway—*mesmerized*. Anita had to get up to shut the door. Vicky heard Anita talking, but her voice sounded distant and muffled. "Girl, what was that all about? Come on, don't hold back. Tell me everything!"

———————— ∼ ————————

Beverly sat with Brandon in an open environment, but she didn't care. It felt warm and cozy to her. Since most of the songs were instrumental, it was challenging for Brandon to sing in his natural voice range, but he tried. He sang very low and tried to sing the melody of the song and not the harmony parts he was used to.

Beverly joined in on "The First Noel", and "Oh Come All Ye Faithful". It surprised them both that they remembered all the words. Brandon weighed his words on how to phrase his next question. "Beverly I don't do this very often, but in this setting with all the festivities surrounding us, would it offend you if I ordered a glass of Champaign?" "No, not at all. It's been years since I've had Champaign. As a matter of fact, an uncorked bottle sits in my cabin right now. I thought about opening it, but I didn't. So, yes let's have a glass of the bubbly. I'm pretty sure it's not a cardinal sin, and our salvation will still remain intact."

They smiled, and Brandon flagged down a waiter. "I think we should open our presents now he said, how 'bout you?" Beverly couldn't believe her eyes when she unwrapped her gift. "This can't be true! Brandon this is my favorite perfume. How did you know?" Rather than saying he was very familiar with the scent because Gracie used to wear it, he said, "I have a nose for nice fragrances." He was telling the truth—at least about that perfume. He could recognize it anywhere.

Brandon told Beverly her gift to him was perfect. He said he was thinking of buying another pair of cuff links for some of his dress shirts before he left for the cruise, but decided to wait until he got back home. The hour was getting late, and just when he was going to suggest they call it a night, Brandon recognized the introduction to the upcoming song. He told Beverly to hold on for a minute. The true romantic he was surfaced once again. He wanted to sing this next song especially to her. It was even close to the key he sang in.

Brandon knew how much Beverly missed her family. He turned to face her, and began to sing.


"Have yourself a merry little Christmas,
Let your heart be light.
From now on your troubles will be out

of sight."
He took one of her hands in his when he got down to the verse:

"Here we are as in olden days,
happy golden days of yore…",

and then looking up he saw a small audience encamped around them. He was so embarrassed, he stopped singing. It was evident that Beverly was so enthralled in the moment, she wasn't aware of them either.

The on-lookers encourage him to finish the song. They promised to join in if he did. Several people took pictures while they all finished the song together. Everyone around the whole area began to clap shouting, hip, hip, and hooray!

What Brandon and Beverly weren't aware of is that one of the ships photographers was in the crowd snapping their picture too. He planned on posting it by Christmas afternoon. If they went to the photo gallery for any other photos, he hoped they would like what they saw. He knew the pictures would create excellent Christmas memories for them.

# Chapter 26

When the roommates awoke Christmas morning they realized the ship had already docked in San Juan, Puerto Rico. Anita announced to Betty and Vicky that she had decided to cut her part of the cruise short. She wanted to go home to spend Christmas with her husband and family if she could get a ticket on any flight leaving out that today. She apologized for any inconvenience, or embarrassment she may have caused any of them while on the cruise. She also confessed that after her dilemma, and their absence last night, she had plenty of time to meditate about the kind of life she was living.

Anita said she could see where her selfishness, and sinful ways had hurt a lot of people, and especially her husband. She was ready to stop some of this nonsense she was doing, and get back to where she belonged—no matter what the ticket cost. She hugged the ladies, and whispered *'Merry Christmas'* in Vicky's ear. She told her she didn't have to repay anything back to her; that the ticket for the cruise was on her. Vicky was speechless!

Vicky rejoiced over Anita's change of heart, but was still in a conundrum over what to do. She knew Kevin would be on that flight leaving for the

United States. Should she tell Anita? If she did, would that cause her to change her mind about going home to be with her husband? And, if she said nothing at all, they were sure to end up on the same flight together. While she was thinking about what to do, Anita left the room to go to Customer Services to see what could be done about getting her off the ship, and on to a plane.

The only thing Vicky could think of was to call Terrance. She rang his cabin. The phone rang twice, and a voice on the other end answered. Vicky's heart skipped a couple of beats. She took a deep breath hoping to collect herself. She explained what was happening. Luckily, Terrance had not seen Kevin yet. He said he was going to be allowed to see him for a short five minutes before he was to be escorted off the ship around 9:45am. It was now 8:30am. Terrance said he planned to go down to security around 9:15, and then he was going to pick her up for Christmas breakfast.

Terrance thanked Vicky, and said he knew what to say to Kevin. The tone of his voice had that certain unmistakable note of authority in it. No doubt he could deliver words of warning to his friend which would imply that if he even tried to speak to Anita, or look her way, he wouldn't hesitate to file charges against him. The cruise line may have done all that was in its jurisdiction to do, but he would let Kevin know he had witnessed the occurrence, and he wasn't sure what legal action he would take against him when he got back home, but if he had to, he would. He told Vicky to wait and see if Anita was able to get a ticket before she shared any information with her.

———∼———

Beverly woke with her mind in a fog. She had tossed and turned during the night. Sound sleep was broken by intervals of restlessness. Had Brandon stirred emotions in her she thought were gone and frozen like the grounds of winter? *This is crazy,* she thought. But, how do you send back into silence feelings that have shown themselves to be alive again? Could she undo the magical connection of the last three days? Could she reset the wonderful warm feeling of holding Brandon's hand as he walked her back to her cabin? *No.* No more than she could extricate the inviting closeness of his strong hug, nor the mannerly brush of his goodnight kiss on her cheek. She felt a twinge of guilt last night when she closed her cabin door and leaned against it, because she wished that the gentlemanly peck on the side of her face had been an embracing kiss on her wanting lips.

Beverly didn't feel the usual slight motion of the ship's movement she had gotten used to. Because of that, she knew the vessel had reached the shores of Puerto Rico during the early morning hours, and it was Christmas Day. She peered at the alarm clock on the nightstand. It was nearly eight o' clock. She and Brandon agreed to spend the day together, starting with breakfast, but he asked if he could first meet her at her cabin before they went. She jumped in the shower, and literally prayed for God's guidance. After she dressed, it seemed a silly thing to do, but instead of spraying perfume from her nearly used bottle, she opened the new bottle Brandon gave her last night. It was the same fragrance, yet in a way she couldn't explain the misty liquid touching her skin caused a transition in her mind. The fragrance made her to think of Brandon this time; not her deceased Ronald.

It was Christmas, so cruise or no cruise, Beverly was still old fashioned in some of her ways. She didn't want to dress up, but she didn't want to dress too casually either. She picked out an A-line skirt, a matching two piece sweater set (one made for all-season weather) and a pair of sling back wedged sandals. She wasn't sure all that Brandon had in mind for the day, but she knew for sure that she wanted to figure out a way to get in touch with her family. *Come to think of it,* she thought, *Brandon's son is traveling with him. He might want to spend some of the day with him.*

The knock at the door interrupted her thoughts. A quick look at the clock let her know it must be Brandon. If not anything else, he was punctual. Beverly glanced around the room to see if everything was out of order. She had already made the bed, and saw that no personal items were lying about. Brandon was just given thought to tapping on the door a second time when he heard the lock click and saw the door handle turn.

Beverly opened the door, and stepped to the side. "Merry Christmas", she said. Brandon took in the radiance of her appearance. "Merry Christmas beautiful lady." Seeing Beverly, he was glad he didn't dress too casually, or go overboard fancy. Brandon's mind flashed back for a few seconds thinking on how Tommy had ribbed him. He was watching him get dressed. "Man! I thought women were the ones who emptied their closets trying to figure out what to wear, but dad you take the cake." It was true. He changed his mind several times. Brandon finally decided on a long sleeve oxford shirt, cuffed dress slacks, and his *Stacy Adams*. He reminded Tommy to join him and Beverly at four o' clock for the Christmas service in the chapel. "Okay Pops. As long as I'm joining you guys for a service, and not a wedding. Tommy laughed! You know, you're looking pretty spiffy there. I can tell you like this woman. Somehow she's brought out the 'old Pop' I used to know. I won't let you down. I'll be there."

A wave of moral modesty crept in Beverly's spirit; and without saying anything, it was almost as if Brandon read her mind. Stepping from the corridor into the room he said, "Why don't we just leave the door on a crack, it'll probably make both of us feel more comfortable." Beverly smiled, and asked him to take the chair at the small round table that held the Christmas plant. Brandon spotted his opened perfume box along with a few small unwrapped packages which may have been given to her by her family.  He smelled the familiar fragrance in the air, and was pleased to surmise she had used from the gift he had given her last evening.

Brandon cleared his throat and stood up. "I guess you're wondering why I asked to come by here this morning before we went to breakfast. Well, it's because I wanted to give you this." He reached in the front pocket of his slacks and took out the postcard-size envelope. He took the two or three steps to where Beverly was seated in the chair at the desk, and put the envelope in her hand. She couldn't imagine what was in the envelope. She thought, *Maybe it's a Christmas card.* She read the writing on the outside of the envelope:

**TO: MRS. BEVERLY SPARKS**
**FROM: BRANDON WOODS**

Beverly kept looking at the note card in her hand. She didn't know what to expect.

"Well, he said, aren't you going to open it?" She opened the envelope, and took out the embossed card. She read it, and then she read it again. "What in the world!" she exclaimed. And, before she knew what she was doing; she found herself on her feet with both arms embraced around Brandon's neck. "Thank you, thank you, thank you", she half whispered and half sang in his ear. "How did you know this was what I needed today?"

Brandon understood that Beverly was very appreciative for the gift, however—again she probably was out of touch with what *that* kind of closeness did to a man. She was clutching him around his neck, and whispering in his ear with soft, sweet sobs of *thank you.* Brandon felt like enfolding her in his waiting arms and bringing forth the kiss he withheld from her last night, but he retained himself.

When it dawned on Beverly what she was doing, she broke her hold and stepped back. She apologized to Brandon. He told her that was okay– that he *rather* enjoyed it. Now, she was embarrassed for sure. Brandon smiled at her coyness. Beverly went to the dresser to get some tissue from the open box. She looked at the embossed card again. It had the ships official seal on it. The wording said:

> **This pre-paid phone card allows the passenger(s) in cabin A-1012 to make ship-to-shore calls to anywhere in the USA, or Puerto Rico up to but not exceeding the pre-paid value of this card in US dollars. $50.00**

"Oh my goodness, Beverly said. I don't know what to say." Brandon walked her back to the telephone at the desk. "I do" he said, "let's start dialing those family members and say "Merry Christmas." Beverly asked Brandon to pull up a chair next to hers. They went through the instructions and then the recorded prompts. In a few seconds the telephone was ringing at Ronald Jr's house.

# Chapter 27

Terrance explained the upcoming situation to the man in charge of the ship's security team. Since Anita was able to secure a ticket, they were going to try and have the two of them seated as far apart as possible. After speaking to Kevin, Terrance went to the ladies' cabin so he could walk with Vicky and Anita to the disembarking area. From there he and Vicky were going to have breakfast aboard ship, and then spend part of Christmas day in Puerto Rico.

Betty sat in the cushioned arm chair against the inside wall of their stateroom. Just a few minutes ago the room was abuzz with the frenzy of Anita's packing, the sobs of goodbyes, and the well wishes for a Merry Christmas for all of them. Now, the room lay still and quiet. Betty had some serious thinking to do, and she welcomed the peaceful solitude. She was not comfortable with how fast things were moving along with Melvin. He seemed to be a nice enough man, but something was putting a check in her spirit, Sure, they had gone to high school together, but this was a man she had not seen for more than thirty years, and to be honest–she hardly knew him back then. Why was he pushing full speed ahead with a woman he barely knew? And, what did that statement about *saving him from himself* mean? She decided to stay in for breakfast, and order room service.

———— ∿ ————

Melvin picked up the phone more than once, and placed it back on the cradle every time. He and Betty had not discussed any plans for today, but he wanted to spend more time with her. He didn't want to spend Christmas alone. The word *alone* rang in his ears. He knew he felt something for Betty, or could it be he thought; *I'm rushing the relationship so I won't have to spend Christmas alone?* It's not that he didn't know Betty was a wonderful person; it's just that he knew he was operating out of a crushed ego. His pride was hurt—yet he couldn't allow himself to *use* a nice lady like Betty to ease his pain. After all, it was his injudicious flesh that got him into his mess in the first place. He couldn't let it rule over him a second time.

Melvin reached for the phone one last time. Guilt was eating away at his conscious. He had to see Betty to explain what was going on, and to ask her to forgive him for putting such a heavy demand on her attention. He had to do it even if it meant she might not want to see him again. He dialed her cabin hoping she was there. He got a little nervous realizing that one of the other roommates could answer the phone, but he didn't hang up. As far as he knew, none of her girlfriends had seen them together, and he wasn't sure if she had said anything to them about seeing him. He heard the short, quick ringtones of the cabin phone. The third ring faded in his ear. *Maybe they're all gone to have Christmas breakfast together.* His spirit began to cower, but he thought he would let the phone ring one more time.

Betty shook herself out of her musing. She realized the telephone was ringing. She sprang from the chair and dashed over to the vanity. Melvin was in the process of lowering the phone from his ear when he heard a somewhat breathless "Hello". He recognized the voice.

—⁓—

Beverly was a ball of emotions. The time on her watch read 8:45am, but her Tablet showed the correct time of **Fri Dec. 25. 9:45a**. San Juan, Puerto Rico was in the AST (Atlantic Standard Time) zone. Puerto Rico did not observe Day Light Savings time like main land United States, so she knew Wayne and Emily's household was alive with Christmas morning chaos. She also could appreciate that in the midst of modern technology and smart phones, some households still believed in having a landline number.

One of the older boys was yelling up the stairs trying to get his dad to come downstairs unaware that he may have only had about three hours of sleep. Emily was trying to coax the rest of the gathering to the breakfast table– especially the younger ones whose heart and eyes were fixed on wrapped packages under the tree. Amid the bustle of excitement Carol heard the faint ring of the telephone. She didn't know how many rings had gone by. She pushed the handle down on the toaster, and ran to grab the extension on the kitchen wall. With the kids' oohing and ahhing around the tree, and RJ grumpily entering the living room, it was less rowdy in the kitchen.

Carol picked up the phone and said "Hello". She had to close off the noise still coming from the living room by putting her index finger in one ear. "Hello", she said again. "Merry Christmas. Surprise!" the voice on the other end of the line said. "What…what, Mama is this you? Quiet, quiet everybody, it's Mama on the phone." Emily, who was at the stove scrambling eggs, froze. The living room emptied out in a flash and everyone gathered around Carol. "Where are you? Did you cut your cruise short? Are you home?" Emily's heart began to pound in her chest. Wayne could see that his wife was about to panic, so he walked over to her, removed the pan from the burner, and set it aside. He put his arm around his wife's waist.  Emily's heart began to race. "Oh my goodness! Carol sang out. Hey you'll, Mama's calling from the ship. She's docked in Puerto Rico."

The kids were jumping up and down shouting, "we want to talk to Grandma on a ship."

Beverly said Merry Christmas to each of her grandchildren, and told them to quickly pass the phone around so each of them would get a chance to talk to her. Wayne and Emily went to the living room and picked up the extension. Carol passed the phone to RJ who was in the kitchen with the rest of the gang. He teased his mother telling her how 'cool' it was that she was calling right from her cabin–that in only four days away from them she was *'Big Balling'* like the rich folks."

Beverly laughed, and asked if Emily and Wayne were close by. Emily's voice was shaking. "Hello Mama. Merry Christmas." Beverly detected something in her voice. "Are you all right dear, your voice sounds a little strange?" Wayne cut in before his wife could say anything. He heard the extension in the kitchen hang up, and heard Carol and RJ trying to corral everyone to the breakfast table.

"Well cruising lady, he said in an upbeat voice, I hope you're having a fabulous Christmas, and taking plenty of pictures." "Yes I am, Beverly said, although I haven't sent you any pictures yet. All of this technology was a bit much to take in all at once." Wayne thought he heard a man's voice in the background saying something about helping her if she needed to send pictures. "Maybe we shouldn't keep you" he said, I know these types of calls are expensive." "Oh, don't worry about that. This is a Christmas present from a friend." A lump began to form in Wayne's throat. "A f-r-i-e-n-d", he said drawing out the word. Emily braced herself against her husband. Wayne changed to phone to his other ear, cutting Emily off from the rest of the conversation. "Yes, and I would like for him to say hello."

Brandon waved his hands in the air, crisscrossing them back and forth to indicate his 'no'. He leaned in to whisper in Beverly's ear. "I don't think that's a good idea Beverly. I don't think your family is"…She cut him off mid-sentence, putting the phone to his ear. "Uh, hello there Mr. Sparks", he fumbled. "Merry Christmas to you and your family. It has been a pleasure to meet such a grand lady as your mother. I hope you all are having a joyous holiday, and I'll help Bev…your mother get some of those pictures over to you while the ship is docked here today. Goodbye."

He pushed the phone back into Beverly's hand. Wayne was dumbfounded. "Hello, hello, are you still there", Beverly said. "Who in the world was that?" Wayne tried to keep his voice steady. "Oh", his mother-in-law said in a nonchalant manner, "That is Mr. Brandon Woods, one of the nicest men I have ever met. But, I think I've used up most of my time. I'll tell you all about it when I get back. Much love to everybody, and tell Carol to pick me up from the airport when my plane lands. Goodbye. Merry Christmas."

With that said, she quickly hung up the telephone, not waiting for his goodbye. Wayne was still holding the phone to his ear, but listening to dial tone. In somewhat of a daze he said, "She hung up." "Well, Emily said, was everything all right? What did she say to you?" He told everyone she was having a great time, and told Carol to check over the itinerary so she would pick her up on time from the airport. The rest he kept to himself.

Brandon eyed Beverly very questionably. "Was there any reason you hung up so abruptly? I would think you had another ten minutes or so left to talk." "Maybe, but I had you to speak to the one person I knew would keep his mouth shut about me meeting someone. I'm sorry, but I was so full of joy, I just had to share it with somebody. I hope you don't mind." Brandon smiled enjoying Beverly's spunk. "Besides, she said, I'm hungry and I sure could use a cup of coffee." She quickly countered with fluttering eyelids and a flaunting smile. How could Brandon refuse?

# Chapter 28

Anita sat on the plane trying to be invisible. She didn't want to talk with anyone and she hoped nobody tried to talk to her. Most of the clothes she owned were either too short, too tight, or cut too low in the neck area. She was glad to have the jacket on she left home with. It was only a three quarter length coat, but at least she was wearing slacks. There was not enough time to call her husband before she boarded the flight, so her only hope for a ride home on Christmas day was to reach him at his mother's house, or call a taxi.

Anita's thoughts floated to Vicky and Terrance. Who would have imagined the two of them getting together? *Leave it to me,* she almost said aloud *to pick the wrong friend.* She told herself to stop thinking stupidly. *You couldn't have had any of those men. You're married! Remember.*

The plane must have been climbing to its projected altitude because her ears were stopped up. She reached for her purse to get a stick of gum, and decided to close her eyes and shut down her mind for the rest of the flight home.

"Hello Betty, this is Melvin." Betty's countenance faded. She knew Melvin would be calling, but she hoped this call was from Vicky or Terrance letting her know that everything went okay with Anita getting on the plane. "Merry Christmas Melvin". "Thank you, he said, and the same to you. Look, I know you're probably going to breakfast this morning with your friends, but do you think I can see you later this afternoon, say for lunch. There's something I want to discuss with you?"

Betty could have told him her friends were already gone, and she was eating in, but she didn't feel like sharing that information. She also wanted to talk with him about where this friend/relationship was going, but she had to finish thinking things through first. "That sounds great, where do you want to meet?"

There was still plenty of the morning left, and because he thought she was having breakfast with her friends, he didn't want to impose on their time together. "How about a late lunch at 'Breezes of the Seas', say around 2:00pm?" Betty agreed. Melvin said he would wait for her at the east entryway by the giant toy soldier. After he hung up the phone, he stood there a while—thinking. He picked the phone up again and ordered from the room service menu.

Melvin looked over the daily newsletter to see what was happening for entertainment on Christmas day. Since they were docked in San Juan most of the shops and boutiques aboard ship were closed. If anyone needed to do a last minute purchase, they would probably have to debark, and find something ashore. He saw there were several times listed for a chapel service. He wanted to go to one of them, however he didn't want to go by himself; which was odd because he'd been going to church alone ever since his divorce.

The theatre would be showing movies most of the day. He looked over the list and saw that there was something to please every palate. Every page printed a reminder that the Casinos, night clubs, and ships Bars were closed Christmas day. They would reopen at 5:00pm. Melvin thought that was only fair. Hopefully those who wanted their Christmas cheer had purchased it before today. The personal service aboard ship didn't seem diminished, but he imagined that some crew workers had a little extra time off, and some may even have planned to meet up with family in Puerto Rico.

———————————⌒————————

Tommy joined his father and Beverly for breakfast. He could see that his dad was very fond of Mrs. Beverly Sparks, and Tommy liked her too. During their conversations Beverly smiled to herself every now and then. It was because Tommy reminded her so much of her own son Ronald Jr. Both men were about the same age, and she couldn't help but think that each of them mirrored what their fathers must have been like when they were that same age. She knew her RJ did.

After a bit, Tommy excused himself from their presence stating he wanted to experience as much of San Juan as he could. The smirk on Brandon's face lent itself to what Beverly was thinking too. They read between the lines. What Tommy wanted to do was to browse around the city in hopes of meeting a non-attached young lady.  He bid them a lovely Christmas. He thanked his dad again for his Christmas gift, and said he would see him later on at chapel.

It seems Brandon and Beverly were on the same page about visiting the island. They would venture out for just a short *looksee*, just enough to say they stepped foot on the island of Puerto Rico. Beverly said she would get a few post cards at one of the open shops near the pier. She wanted colorful pictures to show the family. Brandon thought it was a good idea for them to take pictures standing in front of store shops, and colorful scenic attractions. People offered to take a picture of them standing at those places, and also in front of a blooming flowery display in the middle of the town square. They went back aboard and decided to sit on the deck facing the port. They sat listening to the music coming from the musicians on the pier, and even thought it was Christmas day, a few ladies draped in their colorful native garb, entertained passengers as they meandered back and forth to and from the ship.

The couple decided to go to their cabins to freshen up, and meet in an hour to get a bit to eat from the buffet. After that, they planned to go and see a movie. They would be just in time for 'Miracle on 34th Street". The theatre was showing the updated version, but that was alright with Beverly. She liked the original one she grew up seeing, but at least the make-over kept close to the original story.

When the movie ended they went up to the photo gallery. The pictures of the Captain's Ball, and various setting centered around that night were absolutely breath taking! Beverly wanted everything she laid her eyes on, but she knew she had to limit her longings to a couple selections. The photographers and a few others assumed she and Brandon were husband and wife. In looking at the photos an eerie feeling came over her—*now she could see why.*

"See anything you like?" the voice behind her said. It didn't startle her, and she didn't need to turn around. Beverly was comfortable with Brandon's voice, and *now* his closeness. Her heart pounded as she gathered in boldness and pointed to the photo of her and the man seated with her in a booth in the Atrium on Christmas Eve night. "Yes", she said placing her finger on the gentleman. "I believe I like him." Brandon slid beside her and reached for her free hand. He gave it a gentle squeeze. "And, my *Florence Nightingale,* I believe it's safe to say this man likes you too." He turned to look Beverly square in the face. She was afraid to lift her eyes to meet his. So, Brandon took his right hand and cupped it under Beverly's chin. He cautiously leaned down and brushed her cheek fondly with his lips, but unconsciously continued traveling downward to kiss the rim of her beautiful, soft mouth. It wasn't his plan, but giving *praise* to the *'Season'*—the timing was perfect!

———— ~ ————

Vicky almost had to pinch herself to believe what was happening to her. It was Christmas, and she was sitting in a restaurant in San Juan, Puerto Rico with a handsome attorney. There was no *'Anita's'* around. He wasn't with a group of cronies. He was with her! She looked down at the charm bracelet on her wrist. Terrance had waited until they were seated at the booth near a picture window in the cozy little restaurant, and then put the other small box in front of her. "Merry Christmas Vicky." Vicky was speechless. Not just one present, but Terrance had given her two gifts. The waiter came by to take their order. Not knowing what to choose, Terrance asked the server to select something special from the menu he thought they would enjoy.

Before leaving his room Terrance tore off a section from the ship's newsletter that suggested places to visit for those who were going ashore. The ones marked with an asterisk would be open Christmas day. This was one of the places. A panoramic view of colorful surroundings were at every turn of the eye.

Terrance enjoyed seeing Vicky's face light up with delight each time he surprised her with a gift. The two of them shared more openly about their families and their past Christmases. During the course of their conversation Vicky found out that this wasn't just a Christmas cruise for Terrance, it was also to celebrate his birthday which was on the 26th of December. He said he knew he would have been back home celebrating it alone, so he decided to book the cruise when Kevin asked if he wanted to go.

Vicky asked how the friendship between he and Kevin got started. Terrance told her he actually met Kevin in court. It appears that Kevin needed an attorney for one of his escapade entanglements, and went to the 'Yellow-pages' to find one. Terrance turned up in court as his lawyer. He didn't get him off *scot-free*, but Kevin still wanted to be one his clients. He said that was about five years ago. However, with Kevin's continued shenanigans, the wedge between them had widened, and now with this last caper, he felt it was time to close the attorney/client relationship.

Vicky wondered how this stranger; this man could possibly be so tuned in to what she liked? He didn't know her, yet it seemed he did know her. The jewelry he gave her was exactly what she would have purchased for herself, and this quaint little restaurant/gift shop is something she would have chosen to visit had she been with her friends.

The meal was great. The exotic blends of the cultural cuisine mingled on their palates. The late brunch began with black bean soup and sizzling hot appetizers. They enjoyed _bacalaitos,_ crunchy cod fritters; _surullitos,_ sweet plump cornmeal fingers; and _empanadillas,_ crescent-shaped turnovers filled with lobster, crab, and conch. Even the ginger ale had a kick to it. There was no complaint about the excellent food aboard ship, but sitting in Puerto Rico eating an authentic meal prepared by island residents–was not to be compared to anything the cruise line could offer them. And, besides that, the atmosphere was amazing.

Vicky offered to go _Dutch_ on the meal, but Terrance wouldn't hear of it. A little while after that she excused herself to find the lady's room. She actually wanted to go to the lady's room, but she also wanted to browse through the gift shop. There probably wasn't much there to buy in the way of a Christmas/Birthday gift for a man, but it was worth a look. She spotted their waiter coming from another direction. Vicky explained the birthday situation, and asked if the restaurant could do something in the way of a dessert with a candle on it. He told her not to worry they had something very special for such occasions, and it would be *on the house.*

Coming back from the rest room through the gift shop she spotted two things. One, she knew was perfect for Terrance because she remembered he had a *sweet* tooth, and the other was an attractive cashmere neck scarf. It was tan with burgundy and navy blue lines running through it. She bought a medium size gift bag at the counter to put the items in, and then headed back toward the table.

The waiter was clearing the table when she arrived. Terrance stood when he saw Vicky approaching. She held the bag behind her back with her right hand. He asked if she wanted to order anything else from the menu like a dessert or something. She told him no, she would rather wait until they got back to the ship. There were plenty of desserts on board. He told the waiter to just bring him a cup of coffee and another ginger ale for the lady along with the check.

He excused himself to go to the men's room. When he left Vicky ask the server to wait until Terrance returned to the table to bring the drinks, and then follow up with the surprise dessert. She slid her phone from her small bag, and waited for his return. Vicky was so excited. She had never done anything like this before.

Terrance was thrown for a loop, and so was Vicky. Their waiter came from the back followed by two female servers, and another person who appeared to be one of the cooks from the kitchen. He placed the drinks on the table.  The other servers placed small sized serving squares of traditional _Tembleque,_ chocolate covered strawberry mini cheesecake with gram cracker bottom, and the cook sat a mini mold of Puerto Rican _Coconut Dessert_ sprinkles with nutmeg, in front of Terrance. He then lit the candle, and they all began to sing '_Feliz Cumpleaños_'. Happy Birthday!

Terrance sat with his mouth wide open. "Well, blow out the candle before it melts in the pudding", Vicky said. He could hardly bring his lips together enough to blow out the flame.

Vicky took a few snaps with her phone, and then she put his gift bag on the table. "Merry Christmas and a Happy Birthday!" Terrance's mind was boggled. He tried to finish a complete sentence, but couldn't. "How did you do…? When did…I…I can't believe you…" The servers stood around smiling. But, laughter erupted among them when Vicky said. "He's a lawyer you all. He talks for a living." Terrance had to laugh along with everybody else. The crew left the table singing '_Feliz Nanidad',_ and other customers in the restaurant joined in.

Terrance reached across the table and took Vicky's hand. He was smiling, but his eyes held a glint of moisture in them. "This is the most thoughtful… the nicest thing that anyone has done for me in a long, long time. Thank you Ms. Vicky West. You have made me feel very, *very* special."

# Chapter 29

Melvin stood near the east entry of the open dining room area waiting for Betty. It's wasn't that she was late. He showed up a little early because he didn't want to miss her. His eyes fell on every black woman that exited from the elevator. Melvin knew he had to be sure of what was going through his head. He almost ruined Beverly's opportunity to meet someone special for herself. She was obviously drawn to Brandon—which apparently had not been the case with him. He didn't want to put a damper on the friendship he had with Betty, because he really did like her.

Betty loved the earrings Melvin had given her. She wanted to wear them to show how much she appreciated the gift, but thought it best not to put them on now until she was sure of how far she wanted their relationship to go.

When they met, and began to talk, it seems Melvin had the same idea. In fact, he apologized for his over zealousness, and explained why. Betty understood. The pieces began to fit together more smoothly now. That must have been the woman he eyed more than once at the Captain's Ball. Melvin was honest when he told Betty he really enjoyed her company, and would still like to be her escort to any other upcoming activities for the rest of the cruise–that was if she would allow him.

Betty knew it took a big man to admit his wrongdoings. After all, she was a woman alone on a holiday cruise, and since he was not a stranger—at least not totally, she said she would be honored to be escorted by a thoughtful man such as he. Melvin asked if she wanted to attend the 4:00pm chapel with him. Betty liked the idea. It was already three o'clock in the afternoon, so he said he would meet her at her cabin at 3:45pm.

They left the dining area, and Melvin headed to the photo gallery to purchase a few pictures, especially the one he wanted for the 8X10 frame he bought. When he got there he ordered a second print for himself. Betty decided not to change clothes for the chapel service however, she did add two more items to her outfit; a sweater and the cubic zirconia stud earrings Melvin gave her for Christmas.

———————— ～ ————————

Anita walked through the airport terminal toting her carry-on and her purse. She was so tempted to stop in one of the bars to get a drink. Much to her surprise (and relief) none of them seemed to be open. She wasn't sure if it was because it was too early, or if it was because it was Christmas. Anita read the overhead signs directing passengers to 'BAGGAGE CLAIM'. She still had a ways to go, so she decided to call her husband first. She slowed her pace, and dialed his cell phone. He answered on the second ring.

Anita stopped and moved to the right to get out of the way of the flow of traffic.


"Hello Odie, it's me."
Odis was his given name, but everyone called him Odie.
"Hey Babe. I was hoping you would call. Merry Christmas! Are you still in Puerto Rico?'
"No. I'm here, at the airport."
"What. I thought you had two more days before the cruise ended."
"I did, but…but…

Anita sniffled past the lump in her throat, and tried not to cry.
"Look, I don't want to talk to you while you're over to your folk's house."
"I'm not over my folk's house, I'm home. I've been hanging around here sort of praying that I would hear from my wife."

Anita couldn't hold back her tears any longer. She began to sob softly in her phone.
"Oh Odie, can you please come and get me? I need to…to talk with you. I…I want to…Oh Odie, please say you'll come."
"Okay Babe. Hold on. Just hold tight, I'm on my way. If you haven't done it already, go get your luggage, and I'll be waiting for you outside."

Odis pushed the *end-call* button on his phone. He looked up to the ceiling, and in a joyful loud voice shouted: "Thank you Jesus for my Christmas miracle!"

———～———

Brandon and Beverly attended the four o'clock chapel. Tommy came in, but he sat in the back; not wanting to disturb his Dad and Beverly. The service was a simplistic interfaith gathering. The ship's Chaplain greeted the audience. He announced that if they desired, upon exiting anyone could take one of the souvenir trinket crosses that would be in the containers on either side of the exits.

First he read Isaiah 9:6.7 in the Bible. After that a song '*O Come Emmanuel*' was posted on the overview screen. The music was provided by a pianist, a violinist, and a saxophonist. Next the Chaplain read the Christmas story, Luke 2:1-14. Another hymn was sung, '*It Came upon the Midnight Clear*'. He gave the benediction, and as passengers filed out, music from '*Handle's Messiah*' was played. Some people remained seated to listen and meditate.

Brandon and Beverly sat for a while holding each other's hand. "Well", he said, this has certainly been an unexpected; but delightful experience." Beverly wasn't sure if he was speaking about the two of them meeting, or the chapel service. Brandon continued. "We have the rest of the evening and all day tomorrow to share each other's company." Beverly said, "I know. It seems like a long time, and then again, it seems like no time at all before we…before we", she couldn't bring herself to say the words…*Say goodbye.* Beverly asked Brandon if he wanted to join her for her early dinner seating. He said yes, and agreed to pick her up at her cabin a little before seven o'clock.

Brandon went back to the cabin to see if Tommy had returned. Evidently he had because the room was not as tidy as it was when he left out this morning. There was a hand written note on Brandon's bed. '*Hey pops. I'm back on board. Came to Chapel. Didn't want you to worry. I can't keep up with you. Man your moves are too fast for me! Catch you at dinner.*' *Well,* Brandon thought, *I guess I'd better leave him a note now, because he still won't catch me at dinner.*

———~———

Terrance and Vicky walked a couple of blocks up one side of the street, and turned to their left. He held her hand, and she carried his gift bag. They walked and turned a few more times until they had completed a giant square. Along the way they peered in store windows, looked at the holiday decoration, and took pictures with their phones. After that, Terrance hailed a taxi to drive them the remaining three, or four blocks back to the ship.

Vicky did not complain. However, he *knew* they had been on the move since early morning, and they would need to take a break before dinner. Tonight he wanted to take her to one of the ship's finer restaurants for Christmas dinner. Terrance was aware that Vicky was very self-conscious about her looks, but she would have to get over it, because her looks didn't bother him one bit. He liked her. She was honest. She was a woman of integrity, and she had spontaneity!

Vicky probably didn't even notice that since she wasn't following in Anita's shadow, her appearance and her self-confidence was changing.

Betty turned around when Vicky opened the cabin door. "Hey, where have you been? I thought I might have to send out an APB to find you and Terrance. You *have* been with him all this time haven't you?" Vicky kicked her shoes off and flopped on her bed. "Yes, yes, yes; and it's been marvelous!" She giggled to herself. "I don't know what to do. I can't think straight. This is absolutely the most wonderful Christmas I've ever had." Betty came across the room to stand next to Vicky's bed. She looked down at her friend's face and wiggled her index finger back and forth in the air. "Somebody's falling in love she said in a sing-song voice, and I like how it looks on *her*!"

# *Chapter 30*

Melvin and Betty sat near the front row seats during the chapel service. On their way out, he spotted Beverly and Brandon, who must have come in after he and Betty had already taken their seats. It didn't look as if they were exiting with some of the other passengers. Melvin shook off his fear, and stopped next to where they were seated. He bade them *Merry Christmas* extending his hand to Brandon. He gave introductions all around only hesitating when it came to Brandon's last name. The seated couple returned the holiday greeting adding wishes of hope and peace for the New Year. Melvin felt more at ease. He knew Beverly well, and he could tell that all was forgiven, and she was very sincere in her comment.

Surprisingly enough, Melvin's previous confessions to Betty didn't seem to hinder their relationship at all. Melvin told Betty he felt much more relaxed and she said she felt much more at ease around him, and not so rushed. He was happy to see that Betty was wearing the earrings he had given to her, and that sparked him to ask her to walk with him to his cabin. A questionable expression glinted her face, and he quickly explained that he had another gift he wanted to give her, but it was too awkward to carry around. She gave him one of her quirky half smiles and said, "Well, I guess it'll be alright. A lot of people have seen me with you, and if I turn up missing they know who to look for."

Melvin was caught off guard, and the look on his face showed it. Betty couldn't hold in her laughter a second longer. She burst into a historical laugh catching her breath between wheezes saying, "You should…have seen the look…on your face!" It was so amusing, Melvin had to laugh too. *Hum,* he thought, *this woman has a sense of humor. I like that.*

Melvin slid his ship-n-sail card through the slot, and unlocked the door. He waved Betty through ahead of him, and followed her in, leaving the door ajar. Betty looked around and noticed how neat his room was; not just because the cabin stewards had been in to do their job, but because there were no clothes left on the bed, or hanging on the backs of chairs. His dresser was orderly, and there were no shoes to be seen. She could only guess the shoes must be in the closet.

Melvin offered her a chair and went to the closet to retrieve the other Christmas gift. Betty peeped in the closet when he slid the doors back, and sure enough; she was right. His shoes were in the closet lined up by matching pairs, with the toes facing in. A confident giggle arose in her spirit. *He must have been a military man.* Melvin got the bag from the shelf. He placed it in Betty's hands saying, "This isn't anything great. It's just that some unexpected delights occurred on this cruise, and you were one of them I wanted to remember. I hope you feel the same way too. *Merry Christmas.*"

Betty slid the unwrapped, framed picture out of the bag. It was breath-taking. *It's amazing,* she thought, *how these photographers can make you look. It was magazine perfect.* She thanked Melvin again, and said she was sorry she hadn't given him a present. He eagerly replied, "Oh but you have dear lady. Remember when I said you rescued me from myself? Well, you did, and you have made this cruise a wonderful Christmas experience for me. You gave me the *gift* of your presence. And, that is one of the greatest gifts a single person can experience…the company of another caring person. Thank you Betty."

---

Anita snatched her luggage from the moving carousel, and went to a curbside spot to wait for Odis. Philadelphia was windy and cold, and she felt the icy weather whip through her thin jacket. In the couple of minutes she stood there her hands had already begin to feel numb. Luckily her wait wasn't long. Odis rang her cellphone to ask where she was standing, and the next thing she knew, he was maneuvering the car to where she was. Anita didn't know how to approach him, or what to say. It had been so long since she treated her husband in a civil manner, she was too embarrassed to look him in the face.

Odis turned his flashers on and put the car in 'park'. He jumped out of the driver's seat and headed toward Anita. "Hello", he said in a mild voice. Anita looked at him, but didn't say anything. Instead, she reached for her roller bag. "No Babe, let me do that. You get in the car. You must be half frozen by now." Anita could tell he didn't say it out of sarcasms, but out of genuine concern. He opened the passenger door, and assisted her into the car. Odis loaded the two pieces of luggage in the back seat, and got behind the wheel. "Comfy", he asked, and she nodded *'yes'*.

Anita's eyes filled with moisture. She wanted to say something…to explain, but the words wouldn't come. Anyway she wouldn't know where to start. Odis pulled the car away from the curb, and looked at his wife. "Look Babe, you don't have to say anything. The important thing is that you're safe, you're home, and it's Christmas! We can talk later on, or whenever you feel like it." Anita tried to force a smile through the already trickling tears.

She didn't understand it, but for some reason it seemed as though Odie knew what she had been through. The immense tension she felt beforehand seemed to drain from her body.

She closed her eyes nestling her back against the heated leather seat, and suddenly she felt an aura of protection surround her.

Brandon left his son a note saying that he would be having dinner with Beverly, and later they would probably check out some of the night life aboard ship. He thought about taking her to one of the restaurants for dinner, but decided to wait until he picked her up to ask what she wanted to do. Beverly said wherever they dined it was sure to be extra special, being that it was Christmas night. They could keep their regular seating in the Century dining room or go to the open dinning at 'Breezes of the Seas', or to one of the ship's Café's or restaurants.

They decided to have dinner at Buffet. That way they could sit, sort of alone with each other, and also enjoy selections from the buffet instead of a single ordered meal. Beverly didn't want to glutton, but the Christmas buffet looked fabulous! She knew she would never cook and bake like that had she been at home, so why not indulge? Brandon admitted he wasn't much of a cooking widower. He said he did some cooking, but most of the time he either brought home something from the Deli, or went out to eat.

The two of them talked about different aspects of their lives, their deceased spouses, and their family. However, the unavoidable subject of *their* feelings for each other was bound to come up. Once they expressed what they felt about each other, the next thing was to discuss what to do about it after the cruise ended. The first thing Brandon did was to help Beverly enter his contact information into her Tablet. When he entered her information in his phone, he realized they didn't live that far apart from each other. She lived in Greensboro, North Carolina, and he live in Chesapeake, Virginia. He told Beverly that was less than 240 miles away from him. It was only about a four hour drive, and hardly no time at all if he flew. Beverly was surprised and very pleased to hear that.

They spent the rest of the evening walking hand-n-hand taking in the sights and sounds of the season. Later they walked around the outer deck, and stopped to look at the lights coming from the city. Time slipped away from them, and it was almost midnight when he walked Beverly back to her cabin. This time when he said goodnight, he kissed her—and not by accident. It was very intentional.

# Chapter 31

During the night, Vicky turned over to the soft hum of the shop's motors. She had no idea what time it was, nor how long she had slept. She could hear the light breathing of Betty who lay in the bed on the other side of the room. Her eyes fluttered open, and her heart began to race. She was fully awake now, and she did not dream her evening with Terrance. It really happened!

Vicky wanted to pinch herself, but she was afraid to move. *Please God,* she prayed, *if this isn't You, don't allow me to ever see or hear from this man again. I know what it feels like to be rejected…to be the brunt end of a practical joke— even though this doesn't feel like one. I declared that season in my life was over forever. I'd rather live alone for the rest of my life than to be continually experiencing a broken heart.*

Vicky laid there motionless, and quiet—yet the sleep she woke from could not be recaptured. Her thoughts kept rehearsing the romantic evening with Terrance over and over again in her mind. He was wonderful. In one of the moments when her thoughts were still, an almost audible voice spoke in her head. *"I have this matter of your heart in My hands. Be at peace."*

———————～———————

Terrance woke with a smile on his face. He felt good when he asked Vicky about seeing her when the cruise was over. They shared a lot with each other since their first meeting four days ago, and he knew some of the hurts she had been through. He wanted to change all of that for her, and he prayed that she could find it in her heart to trust him, because he was not like those other guys. If he had anything to do with it, he would see that she was never mistreated again, because today he wanted to ask Vicky to be his lady.

He knew Vicky would probably not warm up to the idea right away, or would try to make an excuse about the distance between them just so she didn't have to accept the fact that someone really like her, and wanted to see her again. So, if she did use that as an excuse to get away from him, he could easily fix that. When he got back home he planned to check with the law firm he worked for to see if they had offices, or connections in the Detroit area. He was single and unattached; moving would be an easy task for him.

———————～———————

When Tommy got in around one thirty in the morning, Brandon was sound asleep. Tommy didn't want to wake his dad, so he decided to shower in the morning. But, it was Tommy who woke to Brandon's stirring about. "Good morning Casanova", he said to his dad. "When I'm in, you're out, and when I'm out, you're in. Do you think I can get a couple of minutes with you? *Wow* Pops! Only four days ago you were complaining about wasting good money on a *silly* cruise, now look at you."

Brandon knew his son was right. Earlier, he said he couldn't see his son spending all that hard earned money on a cruise vacation when they could use it for something else. Brandon thought he would have spent the whole time watching Tommy enjoy himself while he sat around depressed and bored.

He was anxious to see Beverly, but he dialed her cabin to say he was going to spend an hour or two with Tommy. Beverly understood, and said she could use the morning going to the spa. She agreed the father and son duo needed some quality time together. Brandon thanked his son for the cruise. He said he got more than he had bargained for, *thinking about Beverly,* but Tommy had already figured that out.

At breakfast Brandon told Tommy he was seriously considering seeing Beverly again very soon after the cruise. As a matter of fact, he wanted to meet her on New Year's Eve night at her church for 'Watch Service'. That way, he would have an opportunity to meet some of her family, and ring in the New Year with the woman he was (strangely enough) becoming to love.

Beverly's entire body relaxed under the skillful hands of the masseuse. Until then, she wasn't even aware that her neck, shoulders, and upper back was so tensed and knotted. The music, gentle aromatic aromas, and sensual oils seeped far beyond her natural senses, and caused her to slip into a half conscious half-awake state of mind. Beverly felt peace and happiness surround her–not just because of the massage, but because she was happy inside. She knew a lot of that happiness had to do with meeting Brandon.

Laying there, a sudden declining low hit her spirit when she thought of this being their last day together. It made her want to jump off the table, and run to be with him.

———————— ∼ ————————

Odis called his parent's house to let them know that he just picked Anita up from the airport, and they wanted to stay in and talk. He said he was sure she wouldn't feel comfortable enough to join the family for dinner, so they should go on without him. Actually, it was he who wanted to spend Christmas alone with his wife.

Odis didn't want to rush Anita into anything, or to have a conversation that would cause her to feel ill at ease. He offered to fix them a light lunch if she wanted to unpack and freshen up. Anita felt strange. She didn't know how to act around her own husband. She looked around the living room, and saw he had added a few more decorations to what they had started before she left. The house looked great. She wasn't surprised. Odis had always been a well-ordered person.

Odis grabbed her luggage and headed toward the stairs. Looking over his shoulder he said, "I'll put these in the bedroom for you, and head back downstairs to see what I can rustle up for us to eat." Anita tried to make lite of the comment saying, "Oh, you can cook?" The *'old-man'* of Odis would have said, *"I had to learn because you were never around to cook for us."* But instead he said, "Well, I thought I would dabble a little in the culinary arts to add to some of my other *manly* skills." At that point he hurled the suitcases on the bed, and struck one of those masculine physique poses you see *'Body Builders'* do in magazines.

Anita had forgotten how amusing he could be. Odis turned at the door and told her to take as long as she wanted. Anita sat on the side of the bed. She had to smile to herself. Actually she laughed at her stupidity. Odis may have been trying to be funny when he struck that pose, but it only reminded her of the fool she was. That man was a 'hunk'. He was *stacked to the Max!* Odis was six feet four inches tall, had a swagger like Denzel– and the real kick in the head was, he was a faithful husband. *Most women would kill for that, and here she was trying to throw it all away.*

Anita emptied her suitcases and put the dirty clothes aside in a pile on the floor. She took a shower. Her stomach rumbled a few times reminding her of its lack of food. She realized her last meal was yesterday in her cabin. She put on a pair of PJ's, wrapped herself in a cozy bathrobe, and slid her feet into the waiting slippers peeking out from under her side of the bed. *That's funny,* she thought, *I haven't slept with this man for I don't know how long, and he still had my slippers waiting for me on my side of the bed.*

Descending the stairs she smelled inviting aromas rising from the kitchen. Odis had prepared a very appealing brunch. Evidently he was not joking about increasing his culinary skills.

He had placed two large platters on the table. One held pecan Belgian waffles, cranberry-walnut muffins, a small container of honey-maple butter, and two small cups of mixed fruit. The other platter held grapefruit halves topped with a candied cherry, scrambled eggs, sausage links, and bacon. The table was set with Christmas placemats, plates that had matching napkins (paper), and a decorative center piece. Anita felt like she was still on the cruise.

She tried to carry on a pleasant conversation with her husband, but found it hard to look him in the face. After the meal she offered to help clean up the kitchen, and put the leftovers away. Odis did most of the work only asking her to load the dishwasher. When all was done, he suggested they sit for a while in the living room, and celebrate Christmas together. Anita purposely chose the wing-back chair avoiding the urge to sit close to her husband. She was hurting so badly for his comforting touch, she would have done anything at that moment to feel his arms around her. She looked at the beautifully wrapped gifts under the tree. Some were for his family, but she knew he had bought some gifts for her too.

Odis went all-out for Christmas. He was like that for birthdays and Anniversaries too. Anita felt awful that she didn't get him anything at all. She had a mind to get him something before she left, but time ran short, and if she had stayed through the scheduled cruise dates, she would have gotten him something in San Juan today. But, here she sat feeling horrible about the whole thing.

Odis lit a fire in the fireplace. He still had been praying silently from the time he picked Anita up, until now. He turned the TV on to the channel that played Christmas music, and then gave her one of the gifts from under the tree. His phone rang, and he kept the conversation short. When he hung up, he said that was his brother. He told Odis that on his way home tonight, he would drop off the dinner plates their mother fixed for him and Anita, along with the gifts his family sent. Odis laughed saying, it would most likely be containers of everything but the kitchen sink. Anita laughed too, because she knew his family knew how to *throw-down* when it came to big family dinners, especially around the holidays.

# Chapter 32

Christmas night aboard ship was full of fun and excitement. Everything was upbeat and 'popping'. There were parties, a special live show in the Palace Theatre, and the night clubs and Casinos were in full swing. Melvin and Betty had dinner early so they could catch the 7:00pm show at the Palace Theatre. The name of the musical show was "Everything Christmas". It portrayed Carolers dressed in early 1900's costumes, solo artist, and a scene with people actually ice skating on a pond. Betty thought, *'how incredible'!*

They ended the evening by going to one of the Jazz clubs. The musicians mainly played Christmas music. There was a featured female soloist in the club they went to, and the floor was open for dancing. The soloist and the Tenor saxophonist ended their gig with *"Have Yourself a Merry Little Christmas'*. Both Melvin and Betty said they couldn't remember when they had a more memorable Christmas holiday, even on dry land.

It was the ship's 'Day at Sea', but Terrance was too excited to *hover* to the covers. Vicky said *'yes to his proposed offer'.* His mind wandered in and out all night long. His sleep was restless, but it was a good restlessness—if there could be such a thing.

He dressed in his 'active ware', and joined the other early morning joggers on the Sun Deck. When his nerves calmed down, he went to the gym to lift some weights. After his workout he wanted to shower, but he forgot to bring a change of clothes. So, back to the cabin it was. It was only nine o'clock in the morning, but to him it felt like half the day had gone by.

Vicky rang Terrance's cabin hoping she wasn't disturbing his sleep. She wanted to let him know since she and Betty hadn't seen each other much during the past four days, and were going to breakfast together to have a little 'girl' time. Of course he understood. They talked for a few minutes, and decided to meet later on at the library.

At breakfast the lady's filled each other in on how their on-board romances were going. Betty said she felt less pressured and more at ease now that she and Melvin decided to pull back a little and slow down their pace. When she heard Vicky's news, she was about to burst with joy. She was so happy that Vicky finally met someone who cared for her just the way she was—which was *beautiful.*

They chatted about Anita wondering how she
spent Christmas, and hoping she had gone home to
her husband, and not to a motel. The friends shared
more time together by going to the photo Gallery to
browse for newly posted picture. They wanted to
look for additional pictures that reflected the
fantastic time they had on the cruise, but also
decided that each of them would find a photo that
Anita was in. They would make a copy of it when
they got home, and mail her the original so she
could remember the good time they had together as
friends.

～

The Lido Deck was packed with last minute
sun bathers. Some of the women's suits appeared to
be nothing more than a triangle napkin attached to
strings. Beverly held their place at a small table
while Brandon went to the open deck grill to get
their lunch: cheeseburger's and French-fries, and a
soft drink. Beverly thought swim would have been
nice on the last day out. She brought her one-piece
swimming suit along on the cruise, and wore it
when she went to the spa, but she didn't want to
wear it when she was with Brandon. Her Christian
modesty wouldn't allow her to expose her bare
limbs to him in such a worldly manner. It would
have been different had she not met him, or if they
weren't interested in each other in *that way.*

On his way back to their table Brandon slowed his pace to take in the beautiful lady he was with. Beverly was wearing a pair of khaki shorts, a sleeveless button-down blouse, and open toe sandals. She topped off her casual cruise look with a large brim straw hat and over-sized sun glasses. Brandon admired her lengthy legs and her lovely brown skin. She looked absolutely fabulous— hardly the fifty-two years she claimed to be. He noticed how attractive she was in anything that she had worn so far, but this was the first time he had ever seen her in so *little* of her. He felt a flush of embarrassment come over his face knowing he was ogling her femininity.

They watched as Tommy appeared in a group of men as one of the contestants in the on-deck activity. It was called '*The male with the sexiest dance moves contest*'. Some of their moves were very provocative, and you could tell that most of the men entered not because they could dance, but because they thought they had sexy moves.

The contest was judged by the ship's cruise director and other members of her crew. A person was counted '*out*' if you were tapped on the shoulder by one of them. That meant they had to leave the floor. Tommy ended up being one of the last three contestants left for that round.

Beverly playfully leaned over to ask Brandon if Tommy got any of those moves from him. *She couldn't believe she'd asked him that, and neither could he.* "It's been a good while, he said in a drawn out baritone voice, but I believe I can manage most of them." Both of them laughed at their boldness. Tommy came in as first runner up. He strutted over to where they were sitting. In a huff he said, "Man, those people don't know smooth moves when they see them,"

"Oh yes they do, his father said, and they give first prize to the guy that had them!" Beverly and Brandon roared with laughter. They nudged each other on the arm, laughing at Tommy. The young Mr. Woods stood there with an unforgiving smirk on his face and his hands on his waist.

Just then, a young lady approached him saying, "Aren't you the guy who was just in the last dance contest? They should have given you first place." She was wearing a bikini, and was very flirty. Tommy took the bait. His confidence level was boosted, and the last thing they heard as he walked away was him inviting her to a dance club later on that evening to experience first-hand some more of his fabulous moves.

Brandon was contemplating his last evening together with Beverly, and wanted to let her in on his intensions for New Year's Eve, but he decided to wait until later. They spent the rest of the afternoon going to last minute sales in boutiques, and to some of the open vendor areas. Beverly wanted to go back to her cabin to get an early start on her packing. Brandon walked her to her cabin door, and they shared an awkward moment, seemingly in a wavering decision of moral etiquette. They concluded to cut through formalities, an ended up giving each other a light kiss. Brandon said he would pick her up for dinner around 7:00pm.

# Epilogue

The final evening of the Christmas cruise set forth different expectations than what Beverly had expected when she first planned her escursion. She wanted to experience something different, but she never imagined her wintery, uncertain heart to give way to another man's warmth and gental love. When Brandon embraced her for the last time that evening, she actually had tears in her eyes. She'd never thought she would have missed another man as much as she missed had her Ronald. Yet—now she would.

Brandon took his handkerchief from his back pocket to wipe her tears. Beverly wasn't quite sure what he meant when he said she would be seeing him soon enough. She knew he said something about a Valentine date, but that was nearly six weeks away. *Maybe,* she thought, *he is trying to encourage me that the time would go by quickly.* She knew they would be in touch by phone, and by texting, if she could get the hang of it. But how could her longing heart hold out until tomorrow?

Melvin had not spoken with Beverly's daughter Emily. He hoped that when he got home he could explain to her what he was trying to say to her on the phone.  It would be up to her to understand. Anyway, that wasn't the case anymore. Melvin was more than pleased about the way things had turned out between he and Betty. Beverly deserved to be happy. It pinged his ego a little at first, but he knew he could never do for her what Brandon seemed to be doing. Melvin guessed the next hurtle he had to conquer was seeing Beverly at church. He thought about staying home from church for a couple of Sundays, than he changed his mind. That's probably just what the enemy wants him to do.

He had to find out if he had been going to church to see Beverly, or because he need God. He really liked Betty, and he owed it to himself and to her to become a better Christian, a true man of God.

Sitting at the terminal gate waiting for his flight to be called, Melvin took out his cell phone. He browsed through the pictures of him and Betty together. He had selfies, single shots, and pictures of them on the boat tour and at lunch. What was more amazing than that was that he didn't have one picture of him and Beverly together—not one! Yes, Betty was the one. She made him feel good. Before shutting his phone down, he checked to be sure all her contact information was stored. *'Yes'*, he smiled to himself, *she really makes me feel good.'*

⌇

When the ship docked early Sunday morning, Vicky called Anita. She picked up on the second ring, but sounded as if she was in a hurry. Vicky wondered what was going on, it was only 9:00 o'clock in the morning. Anita quickly said: "Christmas went great. I'm trying to get dressed for church. Odie is already dressed. Call me tonight. Bye." Vicky couldn't believe her ears. She told Betty how the phone call went, and both of them were thrilled beyond measure.

Vicky boarded her plane and found her assigned return seat. She put her coat in the overhead bin, and sat next to the window. The seat next to her was empty because that was supposed to have been for Anita. She still was in somewhat of a daze thinking about the wonderful time she had on the cruise. *God is incredible.* Her heart used to be so cold and non-caring toward men–and rightly so. But Terrance changed all of that. She smiled just thinking about his presence. She looked around the craft watching the passengers' board.

Vicky looked probingly at the man coming up the aisle. It's funny, she thought how you can go different places, and see a person who looks just like someone you know from back home, or from somewhere else. The gentleman moved closer, checking his boarding pass for his seat number. He stopped right at her row. Vicky became petrified! It *was* Terrance. "Excuse me Madame. Is this seat taken?" Vicky tried to find her voice. "What…How…What in the world are you doing here?" Terrance pushed his carry-on in the overhead bin, and slid in the seat next to Vicky.

"I traded in my ticket on my other flight for this one." "But, I don't understand." "Oh, I just told them that there was a very important person traveling on this flight whose chaperone got ill, and I had to take the chaperone's place."

"Now I know why they call you lawyers the other word", Vicky said.

"Tsk, tsk, tsk Terrance said as he stretched his arm around Vicky's shoulders, I may have stretched the truth a little about the chaperone, but I surely wasn't lying about the VIP part. Now that you're *'my girl'* that's what you are, and I have to see that you get safely home to your door.

Besides, I don't trust you yet. You may have given me a *'bogus'* address. If I'm going to be *your man*, I've got to make sure I have all your right *numbers*."

# *About the Author*

Heath has the distinctive ability of visually drawing the reader into her character's lives. Using captivating and exciting nuances, there always seems  to be a character of  intrigue who adds an awe inspiring curiosity to the story  line.  Although  people are committed to their  faith,  they often battle  with   right   and   wrong   choices.  Her novels institute Godly principles without interrupting the captivating flow of a true  romantic story. She  upholds the responsibility of abstinence for male and female, and by using life experiences, her experience in drama, twelve years teaching in Christian education, and her studies in  biblical theology, this  author is able to bring  the  Word of God  through the  lives of her picturesque  characters  as  they  search  their  way  through questionable daily endeavors,  rendezvous and  chivalrous  acts which  draw them  to the one  they believe God  has chosen for them.

Printed in the United States

* 9 7 8 0 5 7 8 6 8 3 6 9 0 *